"I need yo[...]
to admit i[...]

Electricity cra[...] the apartment. Robyn felt it, and she knew he did, too, when he trailed a finger down her shoulder. Earlier, while Sean was setting the table for dinner, she'd changed into a short sleeveless sundress. Her outfit wasn't sexy, but that's how she felt every time Sean touched her.

She had to force her thoughts to form, her words to pass her suddenly dry lips. "Things are moving too fast."

"We didn't meet a couple days ago," he pointed out. "We've known each other for years."

Robyn couldn't dispute that.

"I've had feelings for you from day one, but I didn't say anything because I didn't want to ruin our friendship."

"Then why are you here?"

"Because I'm older and wiser, and I know exactly what I want. It's you, Robyn. I won't give up on us," he vowed, lowering his face to hers.

Pressing her hands flat against his chest, she stepped back, out of reach, tried valiantly to keep him at bay. "There is no 'us.'"

"You're wrong. There is."

Robyn opened her mouth, but her protest died on her lips. Before she knew what was happening, Sean grabbed her waist, spun her around and backed her up against the wall.

"I have feelings for you, and I won't stop until you're mine."

Dear Reader,

The best thing about writing the California Desert Dreams series was all of the great telephone conversations I had with Yahrah St. John (*Heat Wave of Desire*, June 2015) and Lisa Marie Perry (*Hot Summer Nights*, July 2015). We didn't know each other prior to writing the series but we instantly hit it off and I now consider them friends. We worked closely together on this project and I hope you'll agree that we hit this miniseries out of the park. ☺

Chef extraordinaire Sean Parker is a force to be reckoned with. The more Robyn Henderson tries to resist him, the more he pursues her. And the night Sean arrives unannounced at her resort condo—with dinner, wine and her favorite dessert—Robyn falls victim to her desires and unleashes her inner passion.

Hence the title of this book.

Heat of Passion is a heartfelt love story, and I hope you enjoy reading it as much as I enjoyed writing it. I listened to a lot of Marvin Gaye and Teddy Pendergrass while writing Sean and Robyn's story, so get ready for a sensual, erotic ride.

I dedicate this book to YOU (loyal readers). Thank you for supporting Harlequin Kimani Romance. Your friendship and encouragement mean the world to me, and with each book I hope to make you proud.

All the best in life and love,

Pamela Yaye

HEAT *of* PASSION

PAMELA YAYE

HARLEQUIN® KIMANI™ ROMANCE

Recycling programs
for this product may
not exist in your area.

ISBN-13: 978-0-373-86413-3

Heat of Passion

Printed in U.S.A.

H HARLEQUIN®
TM www.Harlequin.com

Pamela Yaye has a bachelor's degree in Christian education. Her love for African-American fiction prompted her to pursue a career in writing romance. When she's not working on her latest novel, this busy wife, mother and teacher is watching basketball, cooking or planning her next vacation. Pamela lives in Alberta, Canada, with her gorgeous husband and adorable, but mischievous, son and daughter.

Books by Pamela Yaye

Harlequin Kimani Romance

Escape to Paradise
Evidence of Desire
Passion by the Book
Designed by Desire
Seduced by the Playboy
Seduced by the CEO
Seduced by the Heir
Seduced by Mr. Right
Heat of Passion

Visit the Author Profile page at Harlequin.com for more titles.

You don't choose your family.
They are God's gift to you, as you are to them.
—Desmond Tutu

Chapter 1

The lie rolled so smoothly off Robyn Henderson's tongue she almost believed it herself. "I got tired of being cooped up in the office, so I'm treating myself to lunch," Robyn said, parking her yellow Volkswagen Beetle outside the trendy restaurant praised for its eclectic menu and decor. "I'm checking out the new steak bar near the resort everyone's been raving about."

Kimberly Parker couldn't be fooled. She knew Robyn too well. "You won't even go shopping alone, so there's no way in hell you're eating by yourself at a five-star restaurant. So, seriously, where are you?"

Taking off her seat belt, she listened with half an ear as Kim grilled her about her whereabouts. Kim was not only her boss, but also her best friend. They'd known each other since their boarding-school days at Merri-weather Academy, an all-girls school in Massachusetts.

Robyn's scholarship essay, and letters of recommenda-
tion from her teachers, which highlighted her abilities,
talents, academic history and community service, had
helped her win a scholarship to the prestigious school.
They had bonded over their shared interests, and soon
were joined at the hip.

Robyn loved Kim like a sister and was thrilled they
worked together at the Parker family hotel, the Belleza
Resort and Spa, but she couldn't tell her the truth. Not
if she wanted to keep her job *and* their fourteen-year
friendship intact. The less Kim knew about her LA lunch
date, the better. "Fine, if you must know, I'm meeting a
friend for lunch."

"A friend, huh?" she repeated, her tone filled with
disbelief. "Anyone I know?"

"I'll be back at the Belleza in a couple hours. We'll
talk then."

"No, we'll talk *now*. What's his name? What does he
do for a living? Are you interested in him romantically,
or is he strictly a friend?"

Robyn strangled a sigh. Kim should have become a
lawyer instead of a hotel general manager, because when
it came to unearthing the truth, no one did it better. She
was intelligent and perceptive, and it was times like this
Robyn wished her bestie didn't know her so well. Their
daily habit was to work out and have breakfast poolside,
and because she'd failed to mention her plans to Kim that
morning, her friend was giving her a hard time. Robyn
sucked at lying, couldn't spin a convincing tale if her life
depended on it; she knew Kim could see right through
her. Faced with few options, she did what anyone else
in her situation would do: she lied like a felon with his
third strike. "It's nothing, really, I—"

"Are you meeting Erik? Is that why you're being evasive?"

Robyn's good mood fizzled at the mention of Erik Cutler's name. Thinking about her former colleague—the outgoing finance manager she'd befriended months earlier—made her cringe with shame. How could she have been so stupid? she wondered, overcome with guilt. If not for Kim going to bat for her with her dad, she probably would have been fired.

Blowing out a deep breath, she inwardly scolded herself for allowing her ego to cloud her judgment. What had she been thinking? She should have known better. Determined to put the incident behind her—along with that terse, two-hour meeting she'd had with Kurt Parker—she shook off her thoughts and grabbed her purse off the passenger seat.

"You have to sever ties with Erik and move on." Kim spoke in a sympathetic voice, but her frustration was evident. "He's an opportunist, and you can do much better. You're a smart, successful woman who can have any guy she wants."

If that was the case, I'd be Mrs. Sean Parker.

"Tell me the truth," Kim urged her. "I promise I won't be mad."

"I'm not meeting Erik," Robyn insisted, adamantly shaking her head even though her best friend couldn't see her. "I haven't spoken to him in months, and I don't plan to."

"Then who's your mystery date?"

"A guy I met at a charity event last spring." Another lie, another fresh wave of guilt. As an only child, Robyn considered her friends Kimberly Parker and Gabrielle Royce as family, the sisters she didn't have. She hated lying to Kim, but if her girlfriend knew the truth, she'd be pissed, and Robyn didn't want to upset her best friend.

"How are things going at the office?" she asked, desperate to change the subject. Over the past few months, there had been suspicious incidents at the Belleza. Kim and her parents were certain that someone with an ax to grind was trying to ruin the resort and had contacted the authorities to launch a criminal investigation. "Are you still meeting with detectives this afternoon?"

"Yeah, and I hope they've finally cracked the case, because planning my wedding *and* running the resort under these circumstances is incredibly stressful," she said, her voice strained with tension and frustration. "Would you believe the new front desk manager actually asked me about the curse of the Belleza during our meeting? It took everything in me not to roll my eyes."

Robyn groaned. The Belleza curse was a tall tale that dated back to the hotel's beginnings as the Belleza Inn in the late fifties. Back then, even though there was a lot of talk about an alleged buried treasure on the premises, nothing was ever found. The theory was that anytime someone got close to discovering it, something bad would happen to them. Robyn—like Kim and Gabby—was too much of a realist to put any stock in the possibility that ghosts trying to protect their buried treasure were haunting the hotel. What worried her was that there might be a real, flesh-and-blood person out there trying to destroy the Belleza. Or worse, out to harm the Parker family.

"How does Diego know about the Belleza curse? He hasn't been at the resort long."

"Your guess is as good as mine, but if I was a betting woman, I'd put my money on Jonah." The hotel's old bartender loved to entertain guests and staff with outrageous stories.

"Hang in there, Kim. This will soon be over. I'm sure of it."

"You're right, and then I can devote all my time and energy to my groom-to-be."

Robyn laughed, marveling at how much her friend had changed since meeting her kind, soft-spoken fiancé, Jaxon Dunham.

Seeing the time on her dashboard, she stepped out of the car and activated the alarm. "I have to go. We'll talk later, okay?"

"Just make sure you're at Diva's Beauty Salon by three o'clock. It's our last consultation before the wedding, and I need everyone in the bridal party there."

"How can I forget when you programmed the appointment into my phone?" she teased, unable to resist poking fun at her friend. "Don't worry, Bridezilla. I'll be there."

"Don't hate. Congratulate!" Kim's effervescent laugh filled the line. "I'm so excited about getting married I feel like I'm going to burst. I can't wait to become Mrs. Jaxon Dunham."

And, I can't wait to see your handsome brother!

"Have a good one. I'll see you later." Robyn took out her earpiece, dropped it inside her handbag and adjusted her belted, raspberry-colored dress. It had a modest side split and a loose fit. Robyn wished she was wearing something tighter, something that played up her curves, but Sean had invited her to lunch at the end of their conversation that morning, and changing in the middle of the workday would have raised suspicion. Besides, this wasn't a date. Kim and her older brother, Sean, had been at odds for months. He'd been estranged from his family ever since Kim was awarded control of the Belleza. They'd run into each other at a Colombian restaurant recently, but didn't say more than a few words to each other. Enough was enough. In light of what was happening at the resort, Kim needed Sean now more than ever. Robyn had reached out to Sean, determined to reunite the embittered siblings, no matter what.

As Robyn strode through the parking lot, her conversation with Sean played in her mind. When she'd called to tell him about the suspicious incidents at the Belleza, he'd suggested they meet at a restaurant thirty minutes away from the resort. Ironically, the establishment was near The Pinnacle, the Belleza's competitor, which was due to open at the end of the month. Robyn wondered if his choice was merely coincidental or if something sinister was going on, but she quickly dismissed that last thought. Spotting Sean's car—a sleek, midnight-blue Porsche Boxer with personalized license plates that read CALILUV—parked beside the lamppost, she felt a rush of excitement. At the thought of him, her heart hammered in her chest, and a shiver ran down her spine.

Ignoring the deafening sound of her pulse, she straightened her shoulders and walked purposefully toward the restaurant. The sun was intense, raining down from the sky with unrelenting mercy, but Robyn didn't mind the sweltering August heat. Though she was born and raised in New York and hadn't moved to California until after her college graduation, Robyn couldn't imagine ever living anywhere else. She loved swimming and surfing and spending hours at Laguna Beach, relaxing in the hot sun. But it had been weeks since she'd had a weekend off to enjoy those activities.

"Welcome to The Palms," the hostess said, flashing a pageant smile.

Robyn was struck by the lively ambiance and decor. Framed paintings adorned the walls, decorative vases filled with tulips brightened the space, and waiters in classy white jackets hustled around the dining room, chatting and laughing with well-heeled patrons. Delicious aromas drifted out of the open kitchen, rousing Robyn's appetite. Starving, she couldn't wait to eat and searched the main-floor dining room for Sean.

"Are you dining alone?" the hostess asked.

"No, this gorgeous beauty is with me."

At the sound of a familiar voice—a deep, husky baritone that incited illicit thoughts—her pulse quickened. She peered around the leafy bamboo plant and spotted Sean standing at the bar.

Robyn swallowed hard. He was difficult to miss, and not just because he was the tallest person in the room. The acclaimed chef had soulful eyes, a thin mustache and thick, juicy lips Robyn was desperate to taste again. Sean was thirty-three years old, but his expensive threads gave him a mature, dignified look. He was the sexiest man she'd ever seen in the flesh, but it was his boyish smile that made her swoon. *Good God, he's so dreamy I can hardly stand it.*

Her eyes ate up every inch of him, all six feet three inches. Robyn couldn't stop her gaze from sliding over his broad shoulders, and toned physique. Sean was working the hell out of his charcoal gray suit, and as he strode toward her, she realized he was even more handsome than she remembered. Perhaps quitting his job at the Belleza and getting away from the family fold had been good for him, she thought, returning his smile. Catching a whiff of his cologne, she let the refreshing scent wash over her.

"It's great to see you again," he said.

It is? Seriously? You really mean that?

Sean enveloped her in a hug and kissed her cheek. Heat flowed through her, caused her temperature to rise. Closing her eyes, she reveled in the moment, in his un-characteristic—but welcomed—display of affection. He was a chef in a basketball player's body, and feeling his muscular arms draped around her waist made Robyn tingle all over. His lips felt soft, warm against her skin, and his touch caused goose bumps to prickle her flesh.

"I'm glad you called. This reunion is long overdue."

He released her much too soon for her liking, but she faked a smile to hide her disappointment. "How have you been?" She finally managed to find words to speak.

"Can't complain," he said. "I don't have to ask how you're doing. It's obvious. I didn't think it was possi-ble, but you're even more beautiful than you were eight months ago."

His words triggered memories of fine wine, soft music and passionate kisses that had left Robyn breathless. Choosing to concentrate on the present, not the past, she broke free of her thoughts and took the arm Sean offered.

He winked at her, and a giggle tickled her throat. Robyn chided herself to get it together, to quit making eyes at her best friend's brother. *You're a twenty-eight-year-old woman with a fantastic career and money in the bank, so why do you get nervous every time Sean's around?*

The hostess led them through the dining room, placed the menus on their corner table and sashayed back to her post. Seconds later, a brunette with a thick Spanish accent arrived with water glasses and a bread basket. "Would you like to hear the day's specials?"

Robyn didn't, but she listened patiently as the waitress spoke. The brunette chatted with Sean about the menu, then took their orders before moving on to the next table. Robyn was glad to see the waitress go, to finally have Sean all to herself. She hadn't seen him in months and wanted to catch up with him.

Liar! her conscience shrieked. *You're here for another kiss. Just admit it.*

"I'm glad you called," Sean said. "I've thought a lot about you the last few months."

Then, why didn't you reach out to me? The thought reverberated in her head, but she didn't have the guts to ask.

"I wanted to call you," he continued, "but I didn't think you'd speak to me."

Why? Because we had too much to drink one night and made out like teenagers?

Her thoughts returned to that fateful night. After Kim had been awarded control of the Belleza because of her outstanding marketing campaign, Sean had shown up at her doorstep, drunk and distraught. He'd asked if they could talk, and he'd looked so downtrodden, she'd invited him inside for a cup of coffee. Sean had seemed blindsided by his parents' decision and couldn't believe his dreams of running his family's resort had gone up in smoke. She'd listened as he'd poured out his troubles, and when he'd leaned over and stolen a kiss, she'd shocked herself by kissing him back. Robyn had never thought he'd cross that line, but was secretly glad he had.

The logical part of her mind had warned her to pull back, but her body had yearned for more. His advance had been fueled by liquor, but she'd still felt special, chosen. After all, Sean had had several casual girlfriends who would have gladly hooked up with him that night— or any night for that matter—but he'd come to *her* door and found solace in *her* arms. And it had been the greatest feeling in the word.

Try as she might, she couldn't stop thinking about that sensuous, passionate night. They hadn't slept together, and Robyn didn't know whether to be grateful or sorry about the missed opportunity. They'd kissed and laughed, stroked and caressed each other for hours, but stopped short of doing the deed. It had been the wise thing to do, but part of her secretly regretted not making love to Sean.

No one knew about their late-night hookup, and although months had passed, Robyn still couldn't bring herself to tell Kim about what had happened.

"Are you still mad at me for kissing you?" Sean asked.

"No, of course not," she said with a dismissive wave of her hand. "I forgot all about it."

His gaze darkened, but he spoke in a calm, reassuring tone. "I want to apologize for my behavior that night, and I want you to know that I'd never take advantage of you."

Too bad, because you're one hell of a kisser, and you have the most amazing hands.

"How are things going in your department?" Sean asked, unbuttoning his suit jacket. "Have you hired another event planner, or are you still working like a madwoman?"

"You know it!" Robyn shrieked, hoping to make him laugh. He did, and the sound of his hearty chuckle warmed her all over. "I'm planning several parties, the Dunham Foundation gala, and your sister's wedding, of course. Speaking of which, will you be there?"

A wicked grin claimed his lips. "As long as you agree to be my date."

Feeling her cheeks burn, she picked up her glass and tasted her lemonade. Damn Sean and his megawatt smile. Every time he looked at her like *that*, his gaze blazing with fire and desire, she lost her train of thought. It had always been that way.

That's no surprise, her honest inner voice said. *You've had a crush on him since eighth grade.*

Her thoughts returned to the summer they met, and she pictured the scene in her mind's eye as she sipped her lemonade. She was visiting Kim during summer break, and was in the Parker family kitchen with Kim, baking shortbread cookies, when Sean had walked in, dribbling a basketball. The tray had fallen from Robyn's hands, and cookies had scattered across the hardwood floor. For several seconds all she'd been able to do was stare at the star athlete. She'd tried to regain her composure, to peel her eyes away from his bare chest, but she hadn't had the strength to look away.

Nothing's changed, her conscience pointed out. *You're staring at him right now.*

The waitress arrived with their entrées, and Robyn eagerly dug into her food. The veal was succulent, full of flavor, and the mushroom Bolognese was so delicious she moaned in appreciation. "This is *so* good," she gushed, swirling her fork around her pasta. "I'll have to bring Kim here one day. She'd love this place, especially the cute waiters."

Sean's jaw tightened and lines of tension wrinkled his smooth brow. He was thinking about his sister, no doubt, about how she'd crushed his hopes and dreams. Sensing now was the perfect time to talk to Sean about his family, she put her utensils on her plate and dabbed her mouth with a napkin. "Have you spoken to your parents recently?" Robyn asked.

"Why would I? They made their choice, and I made mine." He picked up his drink, sipped his soda and put it back down on the table. "Tell me what's happening at the resort. You sounded upset on the phone, and my mind's been running wild ever since you called."

She wasn't upset; she was terrified. Someone was after his family, and she was scared Kim was going to get hurt.

Robyn took a deep breath to steady her nerves and told Sean about the misfortunes that had befallen the resort the past few weeks. Individually, none of the incidents were alarming, but taken together they seemed to form a nefarious pattern. The false complaints about the Belleza, posted on numerous travel sites, the fire outside the Ruby Retreat lounge, the waitress who'd fractured her elbow, the cases of food poisoning—all were worrisome. Robyn suspected someone was out to destroy the resort, but she doubted it was Sean. "It's been a stressful time for everyone."

"I can imagine."

He took her hand in his, and relief flooded her body. He was on her side, a sympathetic friend she could confide in, and it felt good having him in her corner. "Some staffers think the incidents are nothing more than the old 'curse of the Belleza,' but your parents believe something sinister is going on. They're taking the matter very seriously and have hired additional security to ensure everything runs smoothly at the resort."

"Damn. I heard Kim's first few months as general manager were off to a rocky start, but I had no idea someone was trying to destroy the Belleza." Sean blew out a deep breath and raked a hand over his short black hair. "Do the police have any leads? Any suspects in custody?"

"They're being tight-lipped about the investigation, but your dad thinks—" Robyn stopped, catching herself just in the nick of time. "Never mind. Forget I said anything."

"Go on, I want to hear what you have to say." Sean wore a sympathetic smile and nodded his head in encouragement. "I won't betray your confidence. You have my word."

Robyn blurted out the truth. "Yesterday your father fingered you to the police."

Chapter 2

Puzzled, Sean furrowed his eyebrows. Her words didn't make sense, didn't add up. Robyn was joking, had to be. He hadn't seen his parents in months, but there was no way in hell his father had fingered him to the police. Not after everything he'd done over the years to make the Belleza Resort a success. Convinced Robyn was pulling his leg, he chuckled agreeably. "Good one," he said, gesturing at her with his glass. "You almost fooled me."

Silence descended over the table, filled the air with tension. Robyn dodged his gaze, wouldn't look at him. The truth hit Sean like a fist to the gut, leaving him dazed and confused. How had his father turned against him? He knew things had been difficult between them, but he'd had no idea they were that bad.

"You have to return to the resort to clear your name," Robyn said quietly.

No way, no how. I'd rather run naked through a burning building.

"Your family needs you," she continued, raising her voice to be heard above the boisterous chatter in the dining room. "Kim's putting up a brave front, but she could really use your love and support right now."

Sean scoffed and shook his head. "My sister has all the answers, and I highly doubt she needs me, or anyone else, for that matter."

Robyn flinched as if she'd been slapped and shot him an incredulous look. "How can you be so cold? Your sister's going through a difficult time. Don't you care?"

He didn't, but he held his tongue. There was no use arguing with Robyn. He was mad at his family, disappointed that his kid sister had stolen the resort out from under him, and there was nothing Robyn could say to change the way he felt.

"You and Kim have always been so close and fiercely protective of each other."

That was then, and this was now. Kim had betrayed him, and he wanted nothing to do with her.

"Do you agree with my parents?" Sean told himself it didn't matter what Robyn believed, that she was just another smokin'-hot woman he was attracted to, but deep down he cared what she thought. They had a powerful attraction, a mind-blowing chemistry he'd never experienced before, and he wanted Robyn in his corner. "Do you think I'm out to destroy the Belleza?"

"If I did, I wouldn't have called you. You're a good guy, Sean, and I know you'd never do anything to hurt the people you love."

Her words heartened him, lifted his spirits, and for the first time since quitting his job at the Belleza, he didn't feel so alone. He felt understood, as if Robyn cared about him, and made a mental note to send her flowers after he returned to the SP Grill. Sean wanted to cook for Robyn, but before he could invite her over to his house for dinner, she dropped another bombshell. One so shocking he almost fell off his chair.

"A security guard said he saw you lurking around the premises just hours before the fire at the Ruby Retreat, and after your father questioned the guard, he contacted the police."

What the hell? This can't be happening. Sean felt as if he'd been kicked in the teeth by a horse, and needed a moment to catch his breath. He gripped his glass so hard he was surprised it didn't shatter into a million pieces. His restaurant was due to open in a few weeks, and if the media found out about the security guard's erroneous story, it could ruin him. "The guard is lying. I haven't been back to the resort since I quit."

"I believe you, and I want to help. Sean, put the past behind you, reconcile with your family and help the authorities catch the bastard who's trying to ruin the Belleza."

"They should be the ones reaching out to me," he argued, struggling to keep a lid on his anger. "My parents screwed me over big-time, and I don't know if I can ever forgive them."

"You're upset. You don't mean that."

"Yes, I do. And, to be honest, I like being on my own and not having to answer to my father about every decision I make." He gave full voice to his anger, didn't censure his thoughts. "I'm tired of living life according to the Parker rules. Look where that got me."

"That got you training at the best culinary school in

Europe and your own restaurant," Robyn shot back. "The next time you feel like bashing your parents, don't, because you sound like a spoiled, ungrateful rich kid."

Sean winced and hung his head. Taking a moment to recover from the bitter tongue lashing, he considered what Robyn had said. She never minced words, always spoke her mind, no matter what. He admired that about her, thought it was one of her greatest character traits.

"Your parents aren't perfect, but they love you and have always been there for you."

Her words gave him pause. Sean thought about his parents, remembered all the great times they'd shared and felt a rush of emotion. To the outside world, the Parkers seemed to have it all—money, success and status—but they had their fair share of problems, too. Still, he had to admit Robyn had a point. His parents had worked hard to build a good life for him and his siblings, and he never forgot all the times his mom had given him advice about girls or helped him with his homework. His relationship with his father had always been rocky, but his mother was his biggest supporter.

"You're right," he conceded, wearing an apologetic smile. "I have a lot to be grateful for, especially you."

"Me?" she repeated, resting a hand on her chest. "But I haven't done anything."

"Thanks for having my back, Robyn. It means more to me than you'll ever know."

"That's what friends are for, right?"

Friendship? That was the last thing on his mind. At least when it came to Robyn. He wanted her in his bed, and he would pursue her until she belonged to him.

At the thought of making love to Robyn, his temperature soared. An erection stabbed the zipper of his pants. It took every ounce of his self-control not to dive across the table and take her in his arms. Their connection was undeniable, so damn strong he couldn't think of anything but kissing her passionately on the lips. At the thought, his pulse raced out of control. For years, he'd tried to ignore their attraction, but after their make-out session, he started seeing his kid sister's best friend in a different light.

Yeah, and now you want Robyn so bad you're drooling all over your Tom Ford suit.

Sitting back in his chair, sipping his drink, Sean admired her creamy skin, the extra long lashes that framed her hazel eyes and her lush lips. Her diamond-stud earrings and silver-cross necklace gave her dress a touch of glamour. Robyn looked like a woman who was born with a silver spoon in her mouth, but nothing could be further from the truth. She'd been raised in the projects in New York City, and was awarded a scholarship to Merriweather Academy boarding school where she'd met his sister. In spite of her humble beginnings, she carried herself with remarkable poise. Though she was five years his junior, she was wise and discerning and he enjoyed spending time with her.

Sean felt an ache in his belly, a thirst only Robyn could quench, and struggled to control his desires. Sean wanted to kiss her again, imagined himself crushing his mouth to hers, but cautioned himself to relax. This wasn't the time or the place, and he didn't want to ruin their lunch by putting the moves on her. Instead, they finished their meal, and over coffee, they just talked. Sean was shocked to discover how much they had in common. They both loved action movies, the great outdoors and spending their days off at the beach. As Robyn spoke, he learned some interesting facts about her. She was an avid surfer, the only person in her family to ever graduate from college and a die-hard Bruce Lee fan. Upbeat and bubbly, she made him forget his problems and laugh out loud at her outrageous stories about the resort.

"How are things coming along at the SP Grill?" Robyn asked, tasting the carrot cake they'd ordered to share.

"Great," he said, bursting with pride. The restaurant was his brainchild, something he'd been contemplating for years, and thanks to the help of several generous investors, his dreams were about to become a reality. "I've put my heart and soul into this project, and I'll do whatever it takes to make the SP Grill a success."

Sean watched Robyn lick the icing off her fork and groaned inwardly, as if he was being tortured. Sweat drenched his shirt. A spark ignited inside his body when their eyes met, causing lust to course through his veins. The blood drained from his head and shot straight to his groin. Did she have any idea how much he wanted her? How much he needed her right now?

"This cake's pretty good, but yours is much better," Robyn said, gesturing with her fork to the plate. "I hope the menu at the SP Grill is filled with your decadent desserts, because they're to die for, especially your chocolate truffle cheesecake."

"I'll be overseeing the day-to-day operation of the restaurant, not slaving away in the kitchen twenty-four seven."

Robyn frowned and poked out her bottom lip. "Why not?"

"The emphasis at the SP Grill is on luxury foods like caviar, lobster and foie gras, but I'm willing to tweak the menu, just for you."

"You'd better," she said, her tone full of sass. "Or I'll take my business elsewhere."

The sound of her laughter brought a smile to his mouth, made him feel better than he had in weeks. "The SP Grill opens on Labor Day, and to celebrate, I'm throwing the biggest bash LA has ever seen."

That's if you're not in jail! joked his inner voice.

Sean refused to entertain the thought and refocused his attention on Robyn. "I'd like you to be my date for the grand-opening celebration," he said, gently stroking her hand with his own. "It's going to be the biggest night of my life, and I want to share it with you."

Her eyes dimmed, lost their warmth, and Sean knew instinctively that Robyn was going to turn him down. They'd had great conversations about life, shared the same values and enjoyed each other's company, so why was she playing hard to get? Or maybe she wasn't playing, Sean thought, swallowing hard. Maybe Robyn was dating someone else. Was that why she was brushing him off? Why she refused to look him in the eye? Because there was another man in her life?

"Are you inviting your family to your grand opening?"

Hell no, he thought, but didn't say. He missed his family—especially Kim—but he couldn't bring himself to call them. "I don't know," he said with a shrug. "Why does it matter?"

"Because they're my employers and you're their estranged son."

Sean raised an eyebrow, gave her a skeptical look. "I don't work at the resort anymore, and furthermore, you're a grown woman who's free to date whoever she wants."

And, by date whoever you want, I mean me!

"I can't attend your grand opening."

His shoulders fell. Sean was disappointed that Robyn wouldn't be at his side on the most important night of his life and wondered if there was anything he could do to change her mind. "Are you seeing someone?" he asked, driven by curiosity.

"No, but under the current circumstances, it wouldn't be right. I don't want to upset your parents, or cause a rift between me and Kim. She's my boss and, more importantly, my best friend, and I'd like to keep it that way."

Sean nodded, as if he understood, but inside he was doing a slow burn. He loved his sister dearly—even though she'd stolen the resort right from under his nose— but there was no way in hell he was letting her control his love life. He'd have to find a way to see Robyn again, away from the resort, and prove to her his feelings were real. In the meantime, he'd earn her trust and romance her, Parker-style.

"I should use the ladies' room before I head back to the resort." Robyn put down her fork, wiped her mouth with a napkin and picked up her handbag. "I'll be right back."

"You can't leave. We just got here."

"No," she corrected. "We got here two hours ago."

Sean checked his Rolex watch, saw the time, and his eyes widened. He couldn't believe it was so late; more surprising still, despite all the work he had to do at the SP Grill, he didn't want to leave. It was true what they said. Time did fly when you're having fun. He'd like nothing more than to spend the rest of the day with Robyn. Talking, joking, kissing—

"I'd better hurry. I have a three o'clock appointment."

"Don't go. I'm having a great time with you, and I want to hear more about your plans for the weekend." Sean cringed when he heard the words leave his mouth and wished he could stuff them back inside. So much for playing it cool. He felt like an ass for sounding desperate and hoped he hadn't blown his chance with her.

"I can't," Robyn said, shaking her head wildly from side to side, a smirk playing on her lips. "If I'm late to meet Kim, she'll beat me up, and I happen to like this face."

He did, too.

Sean stood, pulled out Robyn's chair and watched as she breezed through the dining room, dazzling everyone she passed with her radiant smile. The event planner was sexy from head to toe, and Sean noticed he wasn't the only one admiring her figure. He felt a rush of pride when he saw the other male patrons checking her out. On several occasions, he'd seen celebrity guests at the Belleza proposition her, and to his surprise and relief, she'd spurned their advances. Unlike his ex-girlfriend, Trina Erickson. For Trina, the richer and the more famous the better. In fact, she'd been more interested in rubbing elbows with luminaries than improving their relationship, and her thirst for the good life ultimately had led to their breakup. Sean had learned at a very early age that people didn't care about him, only what his last name could do for them, but Robyn, unlike the women he'd hooked up with in the past, didn't give a damn about his last name or his family connections.

Sean heard someone whistle behind him and glanced over his shoulder. A full-figured woman with frizzy hair blew him a kiss, but he ignored her. He was with Robyn—a titillating beauty who excited him, and he'd never do anything to disrespect her.

Returning to his seat, Sean took his cell phone out of his pocket and listened to his messages. His eyes narrowed, and a scowl twisted his lips. A detective from the Belleza Police Department wanted to meet with him. Sean wanted to prove his innocence and show his parents and everyone else at the Belleza they were dead wrong about him being the arsonist, but he didn't have the time. The SP Grill was opening in a few short weeks and he had his hands full with work. And if he played his cards right, he'd be spending all of his free time with Robyn.

"Would your wife like another mocha cappuccino?" the waitress asked.

My wife? To Sean's surprise, he liked the idea of Robyn being Mrs. Sean Parker, of them living happily ever after in his new five-bedroom dream house. At thirty-three, he'd dated his fair share of women, but Robyn was in a class all her own. And not just because of her killer curves. She was a free thinker, with a can-do attitude and, most important, loyal. Robyn had proved, time and time again, that she could be trusted, and he appreciated having her in his life.

"No, thanks," he said, retrieving his wallet from his suit pocket. Sean opened the leather sleeve, slid a couple hundred-dollar bills inside and stood, just in time to see Robyn approach their table. Taking her hand, he led her out of the restaurant and through the glass doors.

The sun was hot, the air humid and the breeze light. It was the perfect day to go swimming, and if Robyn wasn't in a rush to meet Kim, he would have invited her back to his place. Though he was swamped at work—hiring staff, finalizing menus and meeting with vendors—he was never too busy for Robyn, and he liked the idea of her hanging out at his house. "When can I see you again?"

"Next time you're at the resort, call me, and we'll have lunch."

Sean wore a blank face, didn't let his frustration show. Why would Robyn suggest meeting up at the Parker resort? A place he wanted nothing to do with? He thought hard for several seconds as he tried to remember her weekly schedule. "Since you're off on Thursday, I thought we could spend the day together. We'll hang out at Manhattan Beach, have lunch at the SP Grill, then check out Posh Lounge in the evening—"

"Sean, I'm not off on Thursdays. I work from home. There's a big difference."

"Then, play hooky." He put a finger to his lips. "It'll be our little secret."

"I can't do that. You know summer is the busiest time of year at the resort, and if I don't keep on top of my paperwork, I'll make enemies in the HR department."

"You're beginning to sound like a broken record," he said, leaning against her car door to prevent her from leaving. "Every time I ask you out, you turn me down. That hurts."

Robyn raised an eyebrow as if she was surprised by his confession and playfully poked him in the shoulder. "Sure it does," she said with a sarcastic tone. "You have tons of girlfriends. You don't need me."

But I do. More than you know. You're the only person I can confide in. "Of course I do," he said, his gaze glued to her lips. "You're my number-one girl, and that will never change."

"Sean, you're a great guy, and I value our friendship too much to—"

Driven by need, he captured Robyn around the waist and pulled her to him, right up to his chest. Sean lowered his mouth to hers and stole a kiss. A slow, sensuous kiss that awakened every nerve in his body. It was magic, the best thing to ever happen to his mouth. She tasted sweet, and he was instantly addicted. He felt her shoulders stiffen, sensed her trepidation and, for a split second, regretted his impulsiveness. But then he heard Robyn moan, and he deepened the kiss. The longer they stood there, teasing and arousing each other, the more he wanted her, desired her, ached to have her in his bed.

Electricity crackled in the air, exploded around them like fireworks. He felt it, knew she did, too, when she draped her arms possessively around his neck. On the surface, Sean was calm, collected, in complete control of the situation, but his heart was pounding so loud he couldn't think straight. He loved the way she felt, her body pressed hard against his, her flesh warm and soft in his hands. He stroked her neck, caressed her shoulders and hips. They were in a restaurant parking lot, in broad daylight, not in the privacy of his home, but Sean didn't give a damn. He wanted Robyn to know that he desired her, that he wanted more than friendship, and what better way to prove his feelings than a little public display of affection? Kissing her wasn't enough; he wanted more, needed more. He wouldn't be satisfied until she was in his bed.

Sean heard Robyn's cell phone ring and tightened his hold around her waist. She broke off the kiss and turned away from him. "Sean, you shouldn't have done that," she said, her eyes darting nervously around the parking lot. "Someone from the resort could have seen us."

"I want you, Robyn, and I don't care who knows."

"That was Kim calling. I could tell by the ringtone. I'd better go or I'll be late for our hair consultation." Robyn threw open her car door, slid into the driver's seat and started the engine. "Thanks for lunch."

Before Sean could answer, Robyn was gone, speeding through the parking lot as if her life depended on it. He stood there, stroking the length of his jaw, reliving every moment of that kiss. He needed Robyn in his life and wouldn't let anyone—not even his family—keep them apart. She was one in a million, the kind of woman he'd be proud to have on his arm, and Sean decided, right then and there, that he wasn't going down without a fight.

Chapter 3

Robyn's gaze fell across the flower arrangement perched on the corner of her desk, and a smile tickled her lips. The gift had been delivered fifteen minutes earlier, and she'd been admiring it ever since. The message inside the Hallmark card touched her deeply, made her feel like the prettiest girl in the world, and every time she read the note, happiness bubbled up inside her.

The flowers don't compare to your beauty, but please accept them as a token of my affection, and know that you are always in my thoughts.

The card wasn't signed, but the lavish, colorful flower arrangement could be from only one person—Sean. Admiring the long-stemmed pink roses, she thought about their cozy lunch yesterday and wondered when she was going to see him again. Sean was a sensitive, soft-spoken gentleman, but he had no shortage of confidence. Or sex appeal. He turned heads every time he entered a room and had such an imposing presence women approached him from every direction. He was a dark-chocolate hottie with killer swag, and just thinking about that kiss they'd shared in the restaurant parking lot made Robyn's mouth water. Sean was the perfect combination of bad boy and boy next door, but she appreciated his chivalrous, old-fashioned ways.

Robyn closed her eyes, but she couldn't get Sean—or that kiss—out of her mind. Inhaling the fragrant scent in the air, she ran her fingers along the smooth, soft petals. She wanted to call him and thank him for the flowers, but he was busy preparing for the grand opening of his new restaurant, and Robyn didn't want to disturb him. Later, when she returned to her condo, she'd give Sean a ring. Talking to him made her nervous—even on the telephone—but she was determined to keep it together.

Girl, please, quipped her inner voice. *When it comes to Sean you've* never *been able to keep it together, so just quit while you're ahead.*

Memories of hanging out with Kim and Sean at the Parker family estate filled Robyn's mind. She'd harbored a crush on him ever since they'd slow danced to "Fallin'" by Alicia Keys at Kim's birthday party, but it was nothing Robyn would ever act upon. She didn't want to lose her job or upset her friend. Besides, she and Sean were all wrong for each other. They were both stubborn, opinionated people with fiery personalities, and back when Sean was the head chef at the Belleza, they'd clashed repeatedly.

That's true, but arguing with him only made you want him even more.

Breaking free of her thoughts, Robyn scooped up a pen and flipped open her monthly planner. Enough daydreaming—she had to focus, had to get her head in the game. She had plans with Kim and Gabby that evening, and if she wanted to leave the office by six o'clock, she had to quit fantasizing about Sean—a man she knew she could never have—and get back to work.

Robyn scanned the items on her to-do list and groaned in despair. Contracts had to be proofed, and entertainment booked. The longer she looked at the list, the more hopeless Robyn felt. She had a staff of three in her department, but it wasn't enough. She'd been working ten-hour days all summer and feared if she didn't get some help she'd collapse from exhaustion. That week alone, she'd planned a Moroccan-themed bridal shower, two engagement parties and a book-club luncheon for a hundred women.

Drumming her fingertips on her desk, she considered what to do. One person came to mind, and even though Charlene Vincent had a reputation for being flaky, Robyn decided to ask the restaurant hostess to give her a hand. She had no choice; if she didn't swallow her pride and ask for help, the Dunham Foundation gala would be a disaster. The biggest charity event of the year could make or break the Belleza.

Robyn didn't want to disappoint Kim and her parents. They'd welcomed her into their family with open arms, and even though she'd been raised in the worst housing project in New York, the Parkers never looked down at her or made her feel inferior. After graduating from Merriweather Academy, she'd enrolled in Boston University, and received a master's degree in Public Relations. She'd landed a job at a chain hotel fresh out of university, and although the hours were long, and the accolades were few she'd shined in the assistant program coordinator position. But now, thanks to Kim and her parents, Robyn was living her dream. Robyn glanced at her watch, decided now was the perfect time to track down Charlene and strode out of her office. The beauty and grandeur of the Belleza Resort and Spa never ceased to amaze her. Palm trees and vibrant flowers added to the tranquil ambience of the property, the air held the scent of tropical fruit, and the postcard-perfect views were nothing short of spectacular. The resort had a golf course, a fitness center and a state-of-the-art spa that attracted celebrities from around the globe, but Robyn's favorite place at the Belleza was the pool area whenever she was stressed out, she swam laps in the pool. The moment she dove into the water, her thoughts cleared, and she felt an overwhelming sense of peace.

Her gaze swept the lush, manicured grounds. For the second time in minutes, her thoughts turned to Sean. Even though her heart knew he was off-limits, she couldn't stop thinking about him and found herself wishing he was at the resort. Robyn remembered all the times they'd played tennis and jogged along the trails, talking and cracking jokes. Robyn missed seeing Sean every day and hanging out with him on their days off. Things hadn't been the same at the Belleza since he'd quit, but she'd never admit that to Kim. He was enemy number one, and whenever she tried talking to Kim about making amends with Sean, her friend became defensive and angry. No, she was better off keeping her thoughts to herself.

And while you're at it, keep your lips off Sean, too, her conscience warned.

The Pearl, a five-star restaurant with award-winning food, was the crown jewel of the Belleza Resort and Spa. Robyn was surprised to find Charlene standing in front of the dining room, flirting with a French film star. Fraternizing with guests was against hotel policy, but ever since Kim had got engaged to financial investor Jaxon Dunham, Robyn noticed the female staff were more touchy-feely with male guests—especially the ones worth millions.

"Charlene, may I have a word with you?"

The hostess flashed a sheepish smile. "Yes, of course." Her face covered in guilt, she nervously bit her bottom lip. "What's on your mind?"

"Let's go inside. We'll have more privacy."

Waving goodbye to the actor, Charlene flipped her wavy blonde hair over her shoulders and sashayed into the restaurant with a provocative swish of her hips. She stumbled in her stilettos, and Robyn feared she was going to trip over her feet. Righting herself, she continued through the lounge, smiling wide. Charlene had a beautiful figure, and her slinky, cutout dress drew appreciative glances from several male patrons.

"I can't believe how busy it is in here," Robyn said, noting that every table in the dining area was occupied. The patrons were a mix of silver-haired guests, well-dressed couples and young families. "It's only eleven o'clock."

"Welcome to my world." Charlene glanced around her. "It's been crazy around here all morning. Guests love the new menu, but that's no surprise. Gabby's a whiz in the kitchen."

Robyn felt her cell phone vibrating inside the pocket of her blazer, but she ignored it and gave Charlene her undivided attention. "As you know, I'm planning several high-profile events, and I could really use your help finalizing details for the Dunham Foundation gala and Kim's wedding."

"Sure, why not? I could use the extra money, and besides, I just *love* weddings." Charlene clasped her hands together and swayed from side to side to an inaudible beat. "Who knows? Maybe if I do a good job, Kim will ask me to sing at the reception. Wouldn't that be something?"

Robyn swallowed a laugh. The hostess had a better chance of winning the Mega Millions Jackpot than performing at Kim and Jaxon's wedding.

Charlene had few friends at the resort, but Robyn liked her good humor and positive energy. She could always count on the perky blonde for a laugh, and she was looking forward to getting to know her better. "I know you're busy, so I won't keep you. Just swing by my office after your shift, and I'll fill you in."

Charlene adjusted her dress to reveal more cleavage. "Sounds good, Robyn. See ya!"

A spicy aroma wafted through the dining room, causing Robyn's empty stomach to rumble. Deciding to order a chicken salad, she entered the lounge in search of a waiter.

Stopping abruptly, Robyn narrowed her eyes and hitched a hand to her hips. She was surprised to see Gabby and Kim sitting together at the bar. Why hadn't they invited her for lunch? she wondered, her gaze zeroing in on them like a laser beam. And what was so funny?

Their voices were filled with enthusiasm, and their

excitement was palpable. All business in a fitted black suit, her long black hair cascading down her back, Kim radiated confidence and femininity in equal measures. Just like Gabby. Pretty and petite, the Harvard graduate was often still mistaken for a college coed. Though she was casually dressed in a white T-shirt, skinny jeans and sandals, her beauty was undeniable. Her eyes were striking, her complexion flawless, and her lush auburn curls tumbled around her face every time she laughed out loud.

Robyn smiled at her friends despite her annoyance. They were probably gabbing about their fiancés, she guessed as she headed toward the chatty twosome. That's why they had stars in their eyes and giddy expressions on their faces.

Robyn was thrilled her best friends had met their soul mates, but she couldn't resist teasing them. "Squeal a little louder," she joked, sidling up to the bar. "I don't think the people across the room heard you."

Kim and Gabby burst out laughing and greeted Robyn with one-arm hugs.

"You're not going to believe this." Kim's words fell from her lips in a gush, and stars twinkled in her big brown eyes. "Yesterday, I told Jaxon how much I love sailing, and this morning, I found out he rented a fully staffed yacht to celebrate our two-month anniversary."

Robyn whistled. "Girl, your man's the real deal."

"Tell me about it. I almost fell off my chair when he showed me pictures of the yacht, and he booked live entertainment, too." Kim admired the marquise-cut diamond on her left hand, gazing at the engagement ring adoringly. "Jaxon is the love of my life and, hands down, the most romantic man I've ever met. Sometimes I have to pinch myself to prove I'm not dreaming."

"Me, too!" Gabby shrieked, giving Kim a high-five. "Geoffrey means everything to me, and I cherish every moment we spend together."

Robyn cocked her head to the right, studied her friend closely for several seconds.

Were her eyes deceiving her? Was that a love-struck expression on Gabby's face? The trio had been besties ever since Merriweather Academy—but this was the first time she'd heard her friend gush about someone. "You sound head over heels in love."

"I know," Gabby said, releasing a dreamy sigh. "Isn't it great?"

"I never thought I would feel about a man the way I do about Jaxon, and I wish that kind of love for you, too, Robyn. I hope you find your soul mate and live happily ever after."

Robyn wanted to tell Kim about her feelings for Sean, about how much she enjoyed spending time with him but couldn't. Kim would be upset, and Robyn didn't want to put a wedge between them.

"Have a seat," Gabby said, patting the empty stool beside her. "Take a break."

"Shouldn't you be in the kitchen, whipping up one of your new signature recipes?" Robyn asked, helping herself to a garlic shrimp from the oversize plate and popping it into her mouth. Like everything Gabby made, it was moist and full of flavor.

"I've worked double shifts for the last two weeks, so I'm taking the rest of the day off. I trust my staff, and I know they won't let me down."

Kim spooned sugar into her cup of coffee and stirred. "Robyn, sit, and I'll fill you in on all of the latest wedding developments."

"I have to get back to my office, but you can tell me all about it tonight." Robyn had been looking forward to girls' night for weeks and was excited about spending some quality time alone with her girlfriends. These days, she hardly saw Kim and Gabby—unless they were doing wedding-related stuff—and she missed seeing them outside of work. Jaxon Dunham and Geoffrey Girard were great guys with big hearts, but Robyn was tired of hearing about how wonderful they were. Tonight was supposed to be about reconnecting with her girls, not discussing floral arrangements, seating charts and honeymoon destinations.

"What time are we leaving for the Comedy Store?" Robyn asked. "I'd like to leave early so we can get good seats."

Kim and Gabby shared a puzzled look, shifted uncomfortably on their stools.

"I thought the comedy showcase was tomorrow night," Kim said.

Gabby nodded. "Same here. I must have gotten my days mixed up. Sorry."

"Do you have other plans?" Robyn asked, knowing the answer to the question even before it left her mouth.

"The guys are taking us to The Tower Bar for dinner and dancing."

"You're more than welcome to join us," Gabby added, wearing an apologetic smile.

To watch you coo and fawn all over your fiancé? Been there, done that, and not doing it again! Robyn decided, masking her displeasure by wearing a blank expression on her face.

"I'll tell Jaxon to invite one of his cute investor friends, and we'll make a night of it," Kim proposed. "How does that sound?"

Like torture. I don't do blind dates. Never have, never will.

Robyn felt tears sting the back of her eyes at her disappointment. What was the matter with her? Why was she getting so emotional? Why did it feel as if she was mourning the loss of a loved one?

Because you are, whispered her inner voice. *You lost Kim to Jaxon and Gabby to Geoffrey and now you're all alone.*

Robyn knew she was being ridiculous, but she couldn't change the way she felt. For more than a decade, Kim and Gabby had been her closest friends, and now they were head over heels in love and planning their lives without her. And it hurt like hell. Robyn hated to admit it, even to herself, but she was envious of the relationships Kim and Gabby had, and she secretly wondered if love was in the cards for her.

An idea came to her, one that turned her frown to a smile. Robyn considered inviting Sean to the comedy showcase, even rehearsed what she was going to say when they talked. He'd look great at her side, no doubt about it. Images of him filled her mind. She appreciated being with a man who was not only attractive but intelligent, and Sean was the total package, exactly her type. But they were friends and nothing more, and since she didn't want to give him the wrong impression, she couldn't ask him out.

"Hi, Robyn, how are you doing this glorious morning?"

Jonah Gray, the jovial bartender with the perpetual twinkle in his eye, greeted her with a smile. Eighty-six years young, he'd worked at the resort for decades but showed no signs of slowing down. He was as skillful at handing out advice as he was at mixing drinks and was loved by all. From the time Robyn had arrived at the Belleza, she'd bonded with Jonah. He was a father figure to her, someone she could depend on, and she enjoyed hearing the colorful stories about his past, along with his tales of buried treasure at the resort. "What can I get you to drink?"

"Nothing, Jonah, thank you. I'm not staying."

Kim wore a long face. "Come on, Robyn. Don't be like that. I want to go with you to the comedy showcase, but I can't be two places at the same time."

"We'll hang out tomorrow," Gabby said. "We'll do whatever you want, okay?"

Still, Robyn was unable to shake her foul mood. Feeling her cell phone vibrate, she took it out of her pocket. Her heart skipped a beat when she saw Sean's picture come up on the screen. Her mind raced, jumped from one thought to the next. What was wrong? Why was he calling?

"I have to take this call. I'll see you guys later."

"Who is it?" Gabby asked, her tone filled with concern. "You seem upset."

Robyn stumbled over her words and blurted out the first thing that came to her mind. It was a lame explanation, one she doubted her friends would believe, but she couldn't think of anything else to say. "It's my, uh, mom. She's been having…car trouble, and… I'm worried about her. I'll see you guys at the afternoon staff meeting."

Hustling out of the dining room, Robyn put her cell phone to her ear and spoke in a whisper. "Hello, Sean. Is everything okay? Are you in trouble?"

"No, of course not. What makes you think that something's wrong?"

Sighing in relief, Robyn marched from the restaurant and ducked out one of the side doors. Bikini-clad women, men with perfect bodies and rambunctious children were soaking up the sun and frolicking in the pool. Conversation and high-pitched laughter sweetened the air, and the scent of fresh pineapple made Robyn's mouth water.

"When your number appeared on my phone, I got worried," she explained, feeling embarrassed for jumping to conclusions. "I thought maybe you were in police custody."

"I *am* in trouble…"

Oh God, no! Not Sean. He didn't do what his father is accusing him of.

"I've fallen hard for a pretty event planner from New York, but she won't give me the time of day. Any ideas on how to win her heart?"

Robyn scolded Sean for teasing her. But his soft, sensuous plea and the yearning in his voice made her long to be back in his arms. Her pulse quickened at the thought, and a delicious sensation caused her body to tingle.

Plugging her ear with her finger to block out the noise around her, she listened intently to what Sean had to say. Never before had a man made her feel this way, so special and desirable. He spoke about missing her, about how anxious he was to see her again, and it took everything in her not to confess her true feelings. Robyn pictured him sitting inside his office with his feet propped up on his desk and smiled at the sexy image scrolling through her mind.

"Did you get the roses?"

Robyn nodded her head, though he couldn't see her.

"Yes, I did, and they're beautiful. I was going to call to thank you, but I didn't want to disturb you."

"You could never disturb me. Talking to you is the highlight of my day."

Excited by his words, she rested a hand on her stomach to calm the butterflies within.

"I'm making you dinner tonight," he announced, his tone full of confidence and bravado. "Be at my place at seven o'clock."

Robyn could think of nothing else she'd rather do, but going to Sean's house for dinner was out of the question. She racked her brain for the perfect excuse. Since yesterday, she'd been telling one lie after another, but what choice did she have? If she told Sean the truth—he'd be upset, and Robyn didn't want to lose his friendship. "I wish I could, but I, uh, can't. My car's in the shop, and it won't be ready until next week—"

Robyn broke off as her gaze fell across the couple walking on the pathway. *Damn. Could this day get any worse?* Apparently so, because Sean's parents, Kurt and Ilene Parker, were headed straight for her. They had lunch at the resort every week, so seeing them shouldn't have affected her, but it did. She had to remind herself they had no idea she was talking to their estranged son.

The Parkers were an attractive couple who reeked of wealth and class. Ilene had delicate features, reddish-brown hair and a slender physique that belied her age. Her husband had salt-and-pepper hair and mustache. Kim favored her mother, right down to the way they walked, and the resemblance between Sean and his father was striking.

"I have to go," she said, anxious to get off the phone. She couldn't risk the Parkers overhearing her conversation with Sean, not when they were still furious at him for quitting his job. "I have to get back to work."

"I'm not letting you go until you agree to dinner."

Oh, yes, you are. Robyn thought, trying to squelch her growing sense of fear. She was supposed to be in her office, planning the Dunham Foundation gala, not flirting with Sean—a guy she had no business talking to. She reminded herself that he was a player who collected women like trophies, and Robyn was better off alone than sharing him with someone else.

"I won't take no for an answer, so you might as well give in now," Sean insisted.

Before she could respond, Ilene Parker caught her eye.

"Hello, Robyn," Ilene said with a friendly wave. "If you're not too busy I'd like to have a word with you about Kim's bridal shower."

Robyn's pulse quickened, and her stomach coiled into knots as the couple approached. Feeling trapped, she did something she knew would make Sean mad. She hung up the phone, greeted the Parkers warmly and followed them back inside the resort.

Chapter 4

Sean stood inside the kitchen of the SP Grill, staring at his iPhone, at a loss for words. Had Robyn just hung up on him? He wanted to call her back, but his pride wouldn't let him. He was a Parker, and Parker men didn't beg. Not even for hazel-eyed beauties like Robyn Henderson.

Sean put his cell phone on the counter, scooped up the mail and plopped down on a wooden stool. He'd connect with Robyn later, after he finished his paperwork, and hopefully, she'd be in a better mood when they spoke. Sean wasn't used to her being cold and abrupt with him and wondered if his sister had anything to do with Robyn's odd behavior.

Yawning, he rubbed the sleep from his eyes. Since he'd arrived at the restaurant that morning at 6:00 a.m., he'd been running from one appointment to the next, and it was the first time he'd taken a break. These days, Sean was busier than ever, but he wouldn't trade his twelve-hour work schedule for anything. He was excited that his dreams of owning a restaurant were finally a reality—even if it meant losing sleep. When he wasn't training his staff, he was ordering supplies, overseeing food deliveries and selecting artwork and furniture for the restaurant. His work was never done, and more times than not, he crashed on the couch in his office. But what choice did he have? He couldn't afford to fail. If he did, he would be finished in this town.

He'd never failed at anything, had always pushed himself to be the best; Parkers always did. His worries intensified, and try as he might, he couldn't shake his doubts. Would his grand opening be a success? Would the food critic from the *LA Times* give the SP Grill a favorable review? And most important, would his family show up? Deep down, Sean wanted them to, even if it was just for appearance's sake, but he wasn't holding his breath. They'd let him down before, and he'd be a fool to put his hope in them. Not after everything that had happened since he quit the Belleza.

He felt a sharp pain stab his chest. Yesterday, when he'd had lunch with Robyn, he'd pretended he didn't give a damn about his family, but the truth was that he was miserable without them. He was disappointed in his parents, pissed at Kim for betraying him, but they were his flesh and blood, and life just wasn't the same without them. Thankfully, he still had his younger brother, Ryan. Though he and his musician brother didn't talk often, Sean knew if he ever needed him Ryan would be there in a heartbeat, no questions asked.

Just like Robyn. He glanced down at his cell phone,

hoping she'd sent him a text message explaining her behavior, but no such luck. Sean had his restaurant, his friends and an active social life, but he still felt as if there was something missing. Or rather, someone. For years, he'd secretly lusted over his sister's best friend, but it was never the right time to make his move. But that was about to change. Kissing Robyn at her condo that fateful night then in the restaurant parking lot yesterday confirmed it—she had feelings for him, too.

A grin claimed his lips. The realization made him feel proud, happier than the richest man in the world. Finally, after years of playing the field, he'd found someone special, a woman who'd captured his heart with just one kiss. Because of the earlier, drunken episode, Sean had to convince Robyn he didn't think of her as a "booty call," because she wasn't.

Before they could start a relationship, he had to help Robyn overcome her fears, had to prove that he could be trusted with her heart.

His mind wandered, returned to the night he'd argued with his parents and found solace in Robyn's arms. None of his ex-girlfriends could hold a candle to her, and now that they'd reconnected, he wouldn't let Kim come between them. *Who cares what my family thinks? Our relationship is none of their business.* It was bad enough she'd stolen the resort from him; he'd be damned if he let her ruin his chance with Robyn, too. She was unique, as rare as a ten-carat diamond, and Sean wanted the chance to prove he was the right man for her.

"Here they are! Hot off the presses!"

Sean watched his assistant manager, a petite spitfire named Jolene Warren, march into the kitchen, waving a green piece of paper in the air. Taking it from her out-stretched hand, he peered at the new menu.

"Isn't it great?" she asked excitedly. "It was printed on recycled paper, totally affordable, and the intricate designs on the bottom of the page really make the SP Grill logo pop."

Sean assessed the prototype with a critical eye and realized he didn't like anything about it. It looked cheap, like something you'd see at a roadside diner, and the color scheme was hideous.

"How many menus do you want printed? Two or three hundred?"

"I think we need to go back to the drawing board," Sean said.

"Why? It looks fantastic."

"My last name is synonymous with luxury and class, which means everything associated with the SP Grill has to be lavish and expensive, even the menus."

"But it's environmentally friendly," Jolene argued, hitching a hand to her hip.

"Leave everything to me. I'll take care of it." Sean dropped the sample menu on the counter and stuffed it under the stack of mail he planned to shred. "Did you email the press release I wrote for the media?"

"Yes, and I printed off the updated reservation list, as well. Seventy percent of the dining room is booked for our grand opening, and the cast of *Ex on the Beach* will be here filming that night, too," she said. "I also created a Facebook page for the SP Grill. I hope that's okay."

"That's great, Jolene. Keep up the good work."

A smile brightened her round face. "Thanks, boss. I'm going to go work on the staff schedule, but if you need me, just holler."

His assistant manager exited the kitchen, leaving him alone with his thoughts. Sean wanted to call Robyn back to check up on her, but since he didn't want her to think he was needy, he finished reading his mail, then helped himself to leftovers from the fridge. He'd made lunch for his staff after the orientation session but had been too busy answering questions to eat, and now his stomach was growling so loud he was sure Jolene could hear it in the back office.

As Sean ate, he mentally reviewed his schedule for the rest of the week. He was off tomorrow, and if everything went according to plan, he'd be spending the day with Robyn. The thought made him grin from ear to ear. He could hardly wait. Before yesterday, he hadn't seen her in months, but he planned to make up for lost time. They'd have breakfast at his house, then head to the beach.

Past conversations with his dad, about love and relationships, played in his mind. Sean scratched his head, tried to recall everything his old man had told him about women. What was it he used to say? "Treat a woman like a queen, and you'll always have her heart." With that thought in mind, Sean picked up his cell phone and accessed the internet. He was perusing the Cartier website, searching for the perfect gift for Robyn, when he heard footsteps pounding on the hardwood floor of the dining room. Sean didn't see anyone, but he heard a male voice calling his name and rose to his feet.

Entering the dining room, he searched around for the unexpected visitor with the gruff voice and strong-smelling aftershave. Sean was surprised to find a short heavyset man with tinted glasses, scoping out the bar. "Can I help you?" he asked, giving the stranger the once-over. There was something familiar about the balding, middle-aged man, but Sean couldn't place his face.

"I'm Detective Fenton from the Belleza Police Department."

Damn. It was the detective who'd called yesterday while he was having lunch with Robyn, then again when he was at the gym. Why wouldn't he leave him alone? He had nothing to do with the fire or any of the unfortunate mishaps at the Belleza. He produced a leather wallet, flashed a shiny gold badge and stuffed it into his back pocket. "Are you Sean Parker?"

"Yes, I am. What can I do for you, officer?"

"There was a fire at your family's resort on the afternoon of June 15, and if you don't mind, I'd like to ask you some questions about the incident."

Sean kept his mouth shut, didn't speak. The less he said the better. He watched crime TV; he knew what was up. He had the right to remain silent and would exercise that right if the detective was disrespectful.

"Were you at the resort on the day in question?"

Shaking his head, he folded his arms across his chest and leaned against the bar.

"A security guard said he spotted you on the grounds around noon."

Sean spoke through clenched teeth. "He's lying."

"Is your father lying, too?" Detective Fenton took a notebook out of his pocket, flipped it open and scanned the first page. "Your dad says you're angry at him for awarding control of the resort to your younger sister, Kimberly, and that you're out for revenge."

Sean coughed, but the lump in his throat remained. He was shocked, crushed that his dad thought so little of him. It tore Sean up inside, but he didn't share his feelings with the detective. He kept his voice calm when he spoke. "I was here, at the SP Grill, all day."

Detective Fenton glanced over his shoulder and gestured at the front door with a flick of his head. "I noticed that you have video cameras in the parking lot. Do they work?"

Sean nodded, tried to figure out what the detective had up his sleeve.

"I'd like to see the footage from June 15."

"Sure, no problem. Show me a warrant, and I'll get the video."

His eyes darkened. "Innocent people usually cooperate with the authorities."

Good for them. Sean didn't like the cop's tone, hated his smug, superior attitude. Detective Fenton gave off an angry, hostile vibe, and Sean didn't want to spend another minute in the man's presence. But he couldn't kick him out of his restaurant. Not without making an already bad situation worse.

"I've got twenty years on the job, and I'm a damn good detective. You know why? Because I trust my instincts, and you know what, Mr. Parker? My instincts are leading me straight to you."

Sean's jaw went tight, felt as stiff as barbed wire, and his hands balled into fists at his sides. He'd never punch a cop, no matter how angry he was, but dammit, he was tempted.

"You think you're above the law because you're rich, but I have news for you. You're not," he snarled. "You started that fire outside of the Ruby Retreat, and I'm going to prove it."

Rage bubbled up inside him, threatened to consume him. Detective Fenton was trying to intimidate him, trying to throw his weight around, but Sean wasn't having it. And he wasn't turning over his security video, either.

He straightened to his full height and stepped forward, looking down at the officer. "This conversation is over," he said calmly, despite the anger coursing through his veins. "I had nothing to do with the fire at the Belleza, and I resent you implying that I did."

"Do you know anything about the recent thefts at the resort?"

Sean felt his mouth drop open but quickly slammed it shut. What was he talking about? What thefts? What was stolen? It took everything in him not to ask the questions running through his mind. He knew Detective Fenton was toying with him, trying every trick in the book to trip him up, but he wouldn't give the veteran cop the satisfaction of seeing him sweat. Sean walked over to the door and opened it. "Goodbye, detective."

"I have a few more questions."

Sean wore a broad grin. "Then I suggest you contact my attorney. She's in the book."

"I'll be back, so don't skip town."

Sean watched the steely-eyed detective exit the restaurant and speed off in a late-model gray truck. Thoughts about the Belleza bounced around his brain like the metal ball in a pinball machine. He knew about the fire, the food poisoning, but why hadn't Robyn told him about the thefts? Was there anything else she'd forgotten to tell him?

Sean thought of calling Jonah. Whenever he needed to vent, he reached out to the good-natured bartender, and he could always count on Jonah to give him solid advice. He hesitated as he picked up his cell phone. There was only one person he needed to talk to right now, and it wasn't Jonah Grady.

He hit Redial on his phone and put it to his ear. To his disappointment, his call went straight to voice mail, but when Robyn's smooth, silky voice floated over the line, his scowl fell away. Whatever her reasons for keeping the thefts from him, he knew that she understood, better than anyone, the pressure he was under. Robyn was a lot to handle—fiery, saucy and stubborn—but he liked her. And, assuming his plan worked, he liked the idea of being the only man in her life, the one she'd spend her nights with, the only one she'd make love to.

Sean heard a beep and cleared his voice. "Robyn, it's me. Call me back ASAP."

Hanging up, he checked the time on his phone. Sean was giving Robyn an hour. If she didn't call him back, he was going after her. The thought aroused him, brought a devilish grin to his mouth. He was seeing Robyn tonight, and nothing was going to stop him—not even the fear of being arrested at his family's resort.

Chapter 5

Four o'clock couldn't come fast enough, Robyn thought, glancing at the wall clock hanging above the conference-room door. Once this staff meeting wrapped up, she planned to retreat to her condo, and no one was going to stop her. Kim and Gabby were still trying to convince her to join them at The Tower Bar, but Robyn wasn't interested in meeting Jaxon's investor friend. Instead, she looked forward to a nice, quiet evening alone, eating leftovers and watching TV. Hardly exciting, but it was better than suffering through an awkward blind date. The last time Robyn had put herself out there, she'd been burned, and she wasn't going down that road again. Men were liars who couldn't be trusted, and she was better off without them.

Really? questioned her inner voice. *If all men are no-good dogs, then why did you let Sean kiss you in the parking lot yesterday?*

Robyn told herself not to go there. She didn't want to think about Sean, told herself she was wasting her time. Plenty of women were interested in him—and vice versa—and that was reason enough to keep her distance. Robyn remembered the ever-changing parade of ladies he'd dated in the past, how he'd moved from one girl to the next without a second thought. His last conquest was Trina Erickson, a snobby heiress Robyn had known since her boarding-school days. She'd never liked Trina— still didn't—but there was no denying her beauty. And if Trina couldn't hold Sean's attention, Robyn didn't have a chance in hell of winning his heart.

"That's all for today," Kim said, tapping her pen on the table. "Are there any questions?"

Each department manager was represented at the meeting, a total of twelve people in all, and Kim sat at the head of the conference-room table, consulting her agenda. Like Sean, the staff at the Belleza had been blindsided by Mr. and Mrs. Parker's decision to make Kim general manager, and months later, employees were still adjusting to the shocking news.

"Have you hired additional staff for the weekends?" the housekeeping manager asked. "We discussed it at our last meeting, but nothing's come of it, and I could really use the help."

Kim nodded her head in understanding and wrote on her yellow notepad. "Hiring qualified people takes time, so please be patient. The HR department is doing the best they can."

"It doesn't take three weeks," he grumbled, folding his arms across his ample chest. "If Sean was running the resort, it would have been done already."

Snickers rippled around the table.

Robyn wanted to elbow the housekeeping manager in the ribs for disrespecting her best friend, but she exercised self-control. Robyn stole a glance at Kim. No doubt about it—she was pissed. Her eyes were narrowed, and her lips were pursed, but she spoke in a calm, measured tone, as if she was addressing a child.

"The last few months have been stressful for everyone, what with new management and the mishaps at the resort, and I want you all to know I appreciate your patience and understanding during this difficult time."

Kim stared directly at the housekeeping manager, who lowered his gaze and shifted in his chair.

"Rest assured," she continued, her tone full of confidence. "I'm doing everything in my power to ensure the Belleza remains the number-one resort in California, but I can't do it without each and every one of you."

Robyn was proud of Kim, glad that her friend had taken the high road, even though the housekeeping manager was being a jerk. Her cell phone vibrated, alerting her to a new text, and when she read the message, her heart danced with excitement. Sean wanted to talk and had suggested they have dinner at a five-star LA restaurant known for its tasty cuisine and celebrity clientele. Robyn wanted to see Sean again, but she couldn't do it, wouldn't do it. No good would come of her sneaking around with him. She had to ignore his calls and texts, she decided. She felt bad for brushing Sean off, but she couldn't let history repeat itself.

"Is there anything else?" Kim asked, making eye contact with everyone seated at the table. "Don't be shy. If something's bothering you, speak up."

"I'd like to hear more about the buried treasure and the curse of the Belleza," said the new front desk manager, Diego, his eyes alight with interest. "Any truth to either story?"

Kim shook her head. "Absolutely not. Any other questions?"

"Why haven't the police arrested Sean? What's taking them so long? He's guilty, and everyone knows it, so why hasn't he been locked up?"

Robyn cranked her head to the right and glared at the bony redhead from guest services. All at once, everyone spoke. Questions, accusations and insults flew around the room. Why was everyone against Sean? Had they forgotten all the great things he'd done for them and the resort over the years? It was the first time Robyn had heard employees voice their concerns. She didn't like it, felt as if she was betraying Sean's trust by listening to his former friends bad mouth him. Robyn wanted to leave, but she knew it would look bad, and she didn't want to embarrass Kim.

The stern sound of her friend's voice yanked Robyn out of her thoughts.

"Everyone, please quiet down. Arguing isn't going to solve anything." Kim raised a hand in the air to silence the chatter. "The police are investigating the fire at the Ruby Retreat, but from what I've heard, they're very close to making an arrest. In the meantime, ignore the rumors and focus on doing your job. Remember, our guests are depending on you, and so am I."

Kim was direct; Robyn liked that and inwardly cheered when Kim reminded her staff that Sean was innocent until proven guilty. *Finally! The voice of reason!*

Moments later, everyone filed out of the room, leaving Kim, Gabby and Robyn alone.

"Good job," Robyn said, flashing Kim a thumbs-up.

"I'm glad you set them straight. Sean didn't start the fire and—"

Kim cut her off. "We don't know that for sure."

Robyn exchanged a puzzled look with Gabby, who was standing beside the cooler, refilling her purple water bottle. "You think he did it?" she asked, unable to believe what she was hearing. Confused, she tried to make sense of what her best friend was saying. "But there isn't a shred of evidence against him."

"I don't know what to believe anymore, but I'm sick of talking about it, so just drop it."

Her cheeks heated, and the air grew thick, making it hard to breathe. She felt as if the ceiling was shrinking, as if the walls were closing in on her. "Fine, I won't mention it again," she said tightly, snatching her blazer off the back of her chair. "I'm out of here."

"Sorry, girl. I didn't mean to snap at you." Kim's face softened as she reached out and touched Robyn's forearm. "It's not your fault my brother's a selfish jerk."

He's not a jerk. He's sensitive and thoughtful and an amazing kisser.

"Are you sure you don't want to hang out with us tonight?" Gabby asked.

"I'm positive," Robyn said, nodding her head. "Have fun with your men, and I'll see you tomorrow morning."

Three days a week, Kim, Gabby and Robyn took an early-morning Pilates class at the resort gym. They spent the hour cracking jokes and gossiping about the resort's most colorful guests, and by the end of the session, Robyn felt revitalized. Nothing beat hanging out with her girlfriends and reminiscing about their days at Merriweather Academy—

Nothing? questioned her inner voice. *Not even kissing Sean?*

At the thought of him, a smile exploded onto her lips, and her body quivered.

Thirty minutes later, Robyn entered her condo, kicked off her sandals and collapsed onto the couch. She loved everything about her spacious, two-bedroom suite, just steps away from the pool. The wraparound terrace, the brightly colored fabrics and furnishings and the spectacular views. Simple elegance was the best way to describe the condo, and everything in the suite was eye-catching. Growing up in the projects, surrounded by violence, crime and poverty, Robyn never had dreamed she'd one day live at a five-star resort and rub shoulders with the rich and famous. She was thankful for her mother. If not for her mother working two jobs to put her through school, Robyn had no idea what her life would be like now. Her father had certainly never cared.

Leaning back against the cushions, she closed her eyes and crossed her legs at the ankles. A nap was just what the doctor ordered. Robyn heard laughter and the distant sound of rock music, smelled a spicy aroma that made her mouth water and her stomach roar. Later, she'd warm up her leftovers, but first she needed to rest.

When she heard a knock on the door, she buried her face under a sofa cushion. It was either Kim or Gabby; it always was. Whichever friend it was, she probably wanted to borrow something from her closet or ask her opinion about her outfit. There were upsides to living near her best friends, but being disturbed while she was trying to rest wasn't one of them.

A second knock, louder and longer than the first, forced Robyn up on her feet.

"I'm coming, I'm coming," she grumbled. "Keep your Spanx on."

Robyn yanked the door and gasped. It was Sean! He was there, at the resort, which could mean only one thing. He'd made up with his parents, reconciled with Kim, and now all was right with the world again. Robyn couldn't put her feelings into words, couldn't get her thoughts in order. Joy and relief flooded her body.

"Sean, you're here!" Overcome with emotion, she threw her arms around his neck and held him tight. "It's so good to see you. Welcome home."

Sean gave a hearty chuckle. "Now, *that's* what I call a proper greeting."

"How did things go with your parents? Was Kim receptive to what you had to say? Did you guys smooth things over?"

His eyes thinned, darkened a shade, but his tone was a warm, sensuous whisper. "I didn't come here to see my family. I came here to see you."

Robyn frowned, tried to make sense of his words. It took a moment for her to understand what he'd said, and once she did, her spirits sank. Panic set in, filling her with a sickening sense of dread. A cold chill pierced the air, caused her body to quiver.

Poking her head into the hallway, Robyn glanced up and down the corridor, praying that no one was watching them. Seeing no one, she grabbed Sean's hand and dragged him inside her condo. "Did anyone see you come up here?" she asked, slamming the front door. "Where are you parked? What did you drive?"

"Why did you hang up on me?"

The wounded expression on his face tugged at her heartstrings, but Robyn pretended she didn't hear the question. "Please tell me you didn't drive your Lamborghini here, because if you did, I'm dead meat."

"Robyn, calm down. You're getting yourself all worked up for nothing."

"Nothing?" she repeated, struggling to control her temper. "Are you kidding me? If Kim finds out you're here, my life is over."

"That wouldn't be so bad. You could move in with me and help me run the SP Grill."

Was he going crazy?

"You have the most beautiful scowl."

A giggle slipped from her lips. Leave it to Sean to make her laugh. She couldn't stay mad at him, didn't even try, but she had no choice but to send him away. Feeling a heaviness in her chest, she leaned against the door and released a deep sigh. "Sean, you shouldn't be here—"

"And you shouldn't worry so much."

That was easy for him to say, Robyn thought, annoyed by his laissez-faire attitude. He was born with a silver spoon in his mouth; she wasn't. She needed this job.

"Since you wouldn't come to me, I brought dinner to you."

Sean moved Robyn aside and opened the door. His hands were on her hips for only a second, but his touch wreaked havoc. Her breath caught in her throat, and her temperature soared at the feel of his gentle caress.

"I have everything we need right here," Sean said, holding up a brown wicker basket. "We're going to have fun tonight. I promise."

Robyn sniffed the air, and for the second time in minutes, her mouth watered.

"I hope you're hungry, because I made all of your favorites. Roasted lobster tails, linguine carbonara and a dessert guaranteed to knock your socks off." His gaze captured hers, refused to let her go. Reaching out, he slowly stroked his thumb against her cheek. "I drove all this way for you," he said, his voice a soft, soothing whisper. "You're important to me, Robyn, and I feel connected to you. That's why I'm here. To spend some quality time with my favorite girl."

Her heart softened, turned to mush. No one had ever made her feel so special, so cared for. His words moved her, made her forget her doubts and insecurities. For the first time in Robyn's life, she didn't want to do the right thing; she wanted to *do* Sean Parker.

Chapter 6

"What do you think?" Sean asked, picking up his wine flute and tasting his chardonnay.

Robyn glanced up from her plate and met his piercing gaze. *I think you're sweet and caring and thoughtful, and I'm glad you're here.* From the moment they'd sat down at the kitchen table, they'd been talking nonstop, and Robyn couldn't remember the last time she'd laughed so hard. Everything Sean had made tasted delicious, but what she loved most about dinner was reminiscing with him about their teenage years and all the wild, crazy times they'd had at his family's resort. "Isn't it obvious? I've had three helpings and cleaned my plate each time."

Sean released a deep belly chuckle, and the sound warmed Robyn's heart.

"The linguine was incredible, but you really outdid yourself with dessert," she continued, trying not to gush

but failing miserably. It wasn't everyday Sean—or anyone else—surprised her with a home-cooked meal, and
his kindness touched her deeply. "The cheesecake was
divine, even better than I remembered, and so were the
zuccotto cupcakes."

A proud grin claimed his face. *Handsome* didn't begin
to describe how hot Sean looked in his striped shirt, crisp
shorts and oxford-style sandals. His style was casual but
sexy, and his musky, earthy cologne had a calming effect
on her. She felt comfortable, relaxed, and couldn't stop
smiling, didn't even try. Her feelings were in tumult, vac-
illating between guilt and excitement, but Robyn was determined not to cross the line. Nothing good could come
of her having a summer fling with Sean, and as long as
she remembered what was at stake, she wouldn't have to
worry about getting fired.

"I'm glad you liked everything," he said smoothly,
leaning back comfortably in his chair. "The next time
I come over I'll make you homemade brownies and my
new signature cocktail."

Next time? Robyn struggled with her words, couldn't
get the truth out. There wasn't going to be a next time.
Dinners at her apartment were out of the question. The
risk of getting caught was too great, and Robyn shuddered to think what would happen if Kim spotted Sean
leaving her condo after dark. Would Kim give her a
chance to explain or fire her on the spot?

"It's called California Breeze, and my assistant manager said it's the best drink she's ever had."

"I believe her," Robyn said, nodding her head in agreement. "You're a talented, top-notch chef, and everything
you make tastes amazing."

Sean flashed a boyish smile that made him look years

younger. "Cooking is my passion, what I was born to do, and I couldn't imagine ever doing anything else."

"I know just how you feel. I love being an event planner, and I wake up every morning excited to go to my office and anxious to meet with potential clients."

Robyn forked the last bite of cheesecake into her mouth and washed it down with the rest of her wine. Her gaze returned to Sean's face, zeroed in on his lips. They were moving, but Robyn was so busy staring at him she missed what he'd said. Her confusion must have been clear for him to see, because he frowned and cocked his head to the right.

"You're thinking about work again, aren't you? About your never-ending to-do list."

No, I was thinking about how inviting your mouth looks.

"I hate seeing you like this," he said.

"Like what?"

He appraised her as if she was an exhibit in an art gallery, then reached across the table and took her hand in his. "You've been distracted and jumpy all night."

My frazzled nerves have nothing to do with work and everything to do with you.

At his touch along the inside of her wrist, her body quivered. Robyn couldn't remember ever being so enamored with a man, and wanted to do something wild and spontaneous—with Sean. She wanted to kiss him, to stroke and caress him. Somehow she resisted the desires of her flesh.

"What time should I pick you up tomorrow?" he asked good-naturedly. "I have a fun-filled day planned for us."

"Why don't you hang out with one of your model girl-friends?"

"The only woman I want is you."

"Then you're fresh out of luck, because I have to finish planning Kim's wedding."

A scowl bruised his lips. "These days all you do is work."

"I love my job. Sue me."

"You're a workaholic, and you don't even realize it."

"Takes one to know one," she shot back. "I appreciate your concern, but you're definitely in no position to judge. Back when you were head chef of The Pearl, you routinely put in twelve-hour days and once worked fifteen days in a row."

"I work hard, but I also know how to play hard. Can you say the same?"

"If someone has a reason to throw a party, then they have a reason to hire the Belleza Resort," Robyn said, repeating her personal motto, the one she'd been preaching to her staff for the past three years. "I take great pride in what I do, and I want to make Kim proud. If not for your sister, I'd still be an assistant program coordinator at a chain hotel."

"You got hired because of your outstanding CV, not because of Kim." Sean shook his head, as if he was profoundly disappointed in her. "My sister's got you and everyone else at this resort completely brainwashed, and it's sickening."

Robyn was taken aback by his harsh, bitter tone. She'd never heard Sean bad-mouth anyone, let alone his kid sister, and was surprised by his outburst. Robyn started to speak, to set him straight, but he interrupted her.

"Kim's gone too far this time." He released her hand, took his cell out of his back pocket and tapped his index finger on the screen. "You deserve a day off, just like everybody else, and I'm going to see that you get it."

"What are you doing?" she asked, raising an eyebrow. "Who are you calling?"

"The Iron Lady."

"Who's the Iron Lady?"

"The Belleza Resort's new general manager, of course." Sean put his cell phone to his ear. "You're running yourself ragged planning Kim's wedding while she's off playing kissy face with her fiancé, and that's not fair. She's lucky I don't call the labor board and report her ass for violating the employment standards act."

"No!" Robyn surged to her feet, grabbed Sean's cell phone and pressed the end button. Crisis averted. Releasing a deep sigh, she sank against the kitchen counter, her chest heaving, her heart pounding hard and fast. "Sean, you're wrong about Kim. She works harder than anyone else at the resort, and she's also a fantastic boss, the best I've ever had."

"She paid you to say that, didn't she?"

"Of course not." Robyn had to force herself not to roll her eyes. She pushed his phone out of reach.

"Fine. Keep my cell," he said with a shrug. "I'll just call her from my car."

To keep the peace and avoid Kim finding out about her dinner date with Sean, she said, "Okay, fine, we'll spend the day together."

Triumph gleamed in his eyes. "I thought you'd see things my way."

"Sometimes you're a real pain in the ass, you know that?"

"That's why I'm here. I need a strong woman like you to keep me in line."

"You better keep looking, because the next time you come sniffing around my condo, I'm not opening my door," she joked.

"Yes, you will," he said confidently. "You love having me here, and you know it."

There was no denying it. Sean was right. He was great company and the sweetest guy she'd ever met. They exchanged a heated look, and his stare was so provocative her sex tingled. *If the circumstances were different I would have had Sean for dessert instead of cheesecake.*

"I'd better start busting some suds." He stood, put the dirty silverware in a pile and carried the utensils into the kitchen. "I'll wash the dishes, then make popcorn for the movie."

"Sean, it's almost midnight."

Mischief gleamed in his eyes. "I don't have a curfew. Do you?"

"No, wise guy, but I do have a 6:00 a.m. workout class tomorrow morning."

"Pilates with Kim and Gabby, right?"

"Yeah," she replied, raising an eyebrow. "How did you know?"

"You guys took the same class last summer, and I remember you telling me how much you liked it, especially the cute instructor with the *Magic Mike* body."

Feigning anger, she snatched a butter roll from the bread basket and chucked it at his head. It bounced off the stove, fell to the floor, and Sean chuckled heartily.

"Liar!" she thundered, struggling to keep a straight face. "I never said that, and you know it. Stop putting words in my mouth, or you'll be sorry."

"That's right. I forgot. You're too busy chasing the almighty dollar to date."

It was the last thing Robyn had expected Sean to say, and for some reason, his words hurt her feelings. Was that what he thought? That she cared only about money?

His words made her stop and reflect on her life. Three years ago, when she'd been hired at the Belleza, she'd put in long days and had still had the energy to paint the town red with Kim and Gabby, but her active social life had come to a screeching halt ever since the incident with Erik. Then, just as she was starting to feel like her old self again, her best friends had gone off and found love. These days they'd rather hang out with their fiancés than go dancing at the hottest clubs, which left Robyn stuck at home, watching reality TV. It would be nice to have someone to hang out with, but she'd been burned before, disappointed so many times by the opposite sex that she had given up all hope of ever finding Mr. Right. Her college sweetheart had betrayed her trust, and Robyn didn't know if she'd ever be whole again. But she had to admit. Sean had a way of making her forget everything, and when he was around she couldn't think of anyone *but* him.

"I think I'll pass on the movie," she said, returning the condiments to the fridge. "You like thrillers, but I'm not a big fan."

"I know. That's why I brought *Enter the Dragon.*"

"The Bruce Lee movie?" Robyn felt her eyes widen. "No way. I love that movie."

Sean chuckled. "Yeah, I know, you mentioned it yesterday during lunch."

"I can't help it. It's considered the greatest martial-arts film of all time." Robyn tried not to let her emotions get the best of her, and decided to open up to Sean about her personal life. Maybe if she did, he wouldn't be so hard on his family. He had it good—better than most—and hearing him bad-mouth Kim annoyed the hell out of her. "My dad and I used to watch *Enter the Dragon* every Sunday afternoon. It was our weekly ritual, and I'll never forget sitting on his lap eating chips and drinking soda.

"I've never heard you talk about your dad."

"There's not much to say."

Sean wore a sympathetic expression on his face. "I've opened up to you about my problems, and I hope you'll feel comfortable enough to do the same."

"We used to be close, but…" Robyn faltered over her words and broke off speaking.

Needing a moment to gather her thoughts, she grabbed a towel off the stove and dried the utensils in the dish rack. "My father got remarried when I was sixteen and basically dropped off the face of the earth. He stopped calling and made excuses for why he couldn't come visit," she said quietly. "Our relationship deteriorated further when I was in college. I made a lot of mistakes my junior year, and he's still holding them against me."

"I know how you feel. It's tough not having your father's support, isn't it?"

"Yeah, but I chose to focus on the positives in my life, not the negatives," she said, faking a bright smile. "I have a job I love, amazing friends and family, and—"

"Me." His gaze probed her face. "You'll always have me. You know that. Right, Robyn?"

Robyn melted, could actually feel her heart soften. No words came. She couldn't think of anything to say and stood in silence for a moment, staring at him. His cologne wafted over her, tickling her senses and arousing her body. She wanted Sean, craved his touch, and in her mind's eye, she imagined them making love. The

thought shocked her, made her realize just how bad she
had it for her best friend's brother. Robyn hadn't had sex
in years, not since her college sweetheart had broken her
heart, and she wondered if she even had what it took to
please Sean.

Turning away from him and her thoughts, she bus-
ied herself with wiping down the granite counters. Sean
was suave, more charismatic than any world leader, and
Robyn feared if she didn't ask him to leave she'd lose the
battle with her flesh and end up sexing him on the kitchen
counter. Her feelings were that strong, that intense.

"Thanks for dinner," she said, not looking at him, "and
for sticking around to help me clean up, but it's probably
best that you go."

"Why? Things are just getting interesting."

Robyn paused, considered what to say in response
and decided on the truth. It was time to deal with their
attraction head-on. Sean was the ultimate lady-killer—
smooth, polished, sexy as sin—and she was drawn to
him, desperate for him, despite her fears and misgivings.
But she'd never do anything to hurt Kim. Not after everything they'd been through over the last fourteen years.
She turned to him. "Sean, I like you, but we could never
be more than friends."

"Why? Because of what happened with Erik?"

Her heart stopped dead in her chest. Robyn's knees
threatened to give way, so she leaned against the breakfast bar.

Seconds passed before she spoke, and when she did,
her voice sounded foreign to her ears. It was small, weak,
nothing like her easy, breezy tone. "Who told you?" she
asked. "Was it your old friends from the kitchen staff?"

"No, I ran into Erik this afternoon at the mall, and he had a lot to say about you and Kim."

She'd bet on it, she thought sourly. Erik had got what was coming to him, and she didn't regret anything she'd done that night. Annoyed with Sean for bringing up their former colleague—a man who had zero respect for women—she folded her arms across her chest and returned his penetrating stare. "You shouldn't believe everything you hear."

"And *you* shouldn't put yourself in compromising situations."

His self-righteous tone grated on her nerves, rubbed her the wrong way. "Please leave."

"I'm not going anywhere until you tell me what happened. I heard Erik's side of the story, and now I want to hear yours."

"It's none of your business."

"Yes, it is," he argued. "We have something special, and I don't want a hard-ass like Erik Cutler coming between us."

"I have questions for you, too, then."

"What do you want to know? I'm an open book. I have nothing to hide."

Her home phone rang, and Robyn knew without even looking at the caller ID that it was her mom. Every night, her mother, Laverne, called to check up on her, but since Robyn was dying to get the scoop on Sean's love life, she ignored the phone and asked the question circling her thoughts. "Why did you dump Trina on her birthday?"

"You make it sound so cold and calculated."

"If the shoe fits…" she quipped, trailing off into silence to emphasize her point.

"It wasn't like that."

"Then explain. I'm all ears."

Sean hung his head. He looked pained, as if he'd stubbed his toe, but his voice was surprisingly strong. "We got into an argument during dinner, and when Trina demanded I propose by Christmas, I decided to call it quits."

Silently she applauded Sean. Trina was a self-righteous snob with a funky attitude, and he could do better.

With you, right? her conscience asked. *Tell him how you feel. How much you want him.*

"Erik told me you had him fired," Sean said. "Any truth to that?"

"He's lying. His overinflated ego led to his demise, not me."

"Were you lovers?"

"Hell to the no!" Robyn shrieked, dismissing his question with a flick of her hands. "Erik invited me to his high school reunion, and I said yes."

"Why?" Sean wore an incredulous expression on his face, stared at her as if she'd just confessed to moonlighting as an exotic dancer. "You guys used to butt heads constantly during the staff meetings, and you once called him a six-foot-two crybaby."

"I thought attending his reunion would be a great networking opportunity, and I was right. I told everyone I met about the resort, including an attorney to the stars and several pro athletes, and handed out hundreds of business cards."

"It sounds like the night was a success."

"It was, until Erik tried to kiss me. I turned him down, and he...got rough with me."

His eyes darkened, and he spoke through clenched teeth. "What did he do?"

"I don't want to go into the details," she said quietly, fiddling with her silver thumb ring. "I was upset when I left his suite and confided in Gabby about what happened. Word got back to Kim, and she fired Erik the next day. He went to your father and accused me of setting him up."

"What a jerk," he raged, anger blazing in his deep brown eyes. "If I knew where he lived, I'd drive over there and kick his ass."

"Fighting doesn't solve anything."

"You're right, it doesn't, but guys like Erik deserve a taste of their own medicine."

"Don't worry, I put my self-defense training to good use. When Erik grabbed my hair, I kneed him so hard in the groin he fell to the ground like a sack of potatoes."

"You are *such* a New Yorker," he teased, wrapping his arms around her waist.

"And proud of it."

His touch, along her neck, shoulders and hips, excited her. Robyn was amused by his teasing, turned on by his caress and hungry for one of his slow, sensuous French kisses.

"I'm glad you're okay. I don't know what I'd do if something ever happened to you."

Unable to resist, Robyn snuggled against him and inhaled his scent. Being in his arms was amazing, and she relished the quiet, intimate moment they were sharing.

"Now that I know what went down with Erik, everything makes sense."

His words confused her. "What are you talking about?"

"Your reluctance to date," he replied, tightening his hold around her waist. "You're afraid of getting hurt. That's why you keep pushing me away."

You'd be scared, too, if you had a horrible track record with the opposite sex.

"I'm nothing like Erik. I respect women. I don't hurt or abuse them."

Robyn stepped toward him, gave herself permission to caress his shoulders. Her temperature soared to unimaginable heights when he brushed his lips ever so gently against her cheek. "You have no idea what you do to me. I want you so bad it's killing me inside."

"Kim would never forgive me for—"

"Screw Kim. She doesn't know shit about loyalty."

Robyn dropped her hands at her sides and examined Sean's face. His steely glare and the bitter contempt in his voice troubled her. Then it struck her—why he'd brought her dinner, why he was pursuing her, why he wouldn't take no for an answer. She felt horrible for even thinking it, guilty for lumping Sean in with all the other no-good men in her past, but the truth was staring right in her face. It was so glaringly obvious she wondered why she hadn't figured it out sooner.

"This isn't about me," she said, as all the pieces of the puzzle began to fit. "This is about you and your need for revenge. You're using me to get back at Kim. Just admit it."

"Are you out of your damn mind?"

Robyn glared back at him, didn't wither under his intense stare. "Don't talk to me like that. I'm not one of the bimbos you routinely hook up with, and I won't let you disrespect me."

"I'm sorry," he said quietly.

Robyn stared at him, unsure of what to do next. Then he touched her, tenderly brushed his fingers against her cheek, and her anger dissolved.

"Let me make myself perfectly clear, so there's no confusion later. My feelings for you have nothing to do with Kim, my parents or the resort." He spoke softly, with such genuine emotion, her ears perked up. "I need you in my life, and I'm not afraid to admit it."

Electricity crackled in the air, engulfed every inch of the apartment. Robyn felt it, and she knew he did, too, when he trailed a finger down her shoulder. Earlier, while Sean was setting the table for dinner, she'd changed into a short, sleeveless sundress. Her outfit wasn't sexy, but that's how she felt every time Sean touched her.

She had to force her thoughts to form, her words to pass her suddenly dry lips. "Things are moving too fast."

"We didn't meet a couple days ago," he pointed out. "We've know each other for years."

Robyn couldn't dispute that.

"I've had feelings for you from day one, but I didn't say anything because I didn't want to ruin our friendship."

"Then why are you here?"

"Because I'm older and wiser, and I know exactly what I want. It's you, Robyn."

Sure you do, until someone prettier and sexier catches your eye.

"I won't give up on us," he vowed, lowering his face to hers.

Pressing her hands flat against his chest, she stepped back, out of reach, tried valiantly to keep him at bay. "There is no 'us.'"

"You're wrong. There is."

Robyn opened her mouth, but her protest died on her lips. Before she knew what was happening, Sean grabbed her waist, spun her around and backed her up against the wall.

"I have feelings for you, and I won't stop until you're mine."

Chapter 7

The kiss was a hard, sensual assault on Robyn's mouth, but she didn't pull away from Sean. It was a perfect kiss, a wonderful surprise. She'd been secretly lusting after him for years—ever since the first time they met—and she wouldn't trade being in his arms for anything.

Goose bumps spread like wildfire across her flesh as his tongue slid inside her mouth. Her brain quit working, and all she could do was feel. She was running on pure emotion, and her body was aflame, a raging inferno that couldn't be contained. Robyn felt alive, more desirable than ever before, and Sean was the reason why. She'd never been kissed with such passion, such hunger, and she was so overwhelmed by her emotions she moaned into his mouth.

"You're beautiful," Sean praised between kisses. "A breathtaking masterpiece."

"You're just saying that to get into my panties." Robyn felt her eyes widen and heat stain her cheeks. Had those words actually come out of her mouth? She'd answered without thinking and regretted her saucy quip the moment it reached her ears.

"Keep talking dirty, and I'll spank you for being a bad girl."

Meeting his smoldering gaze, she flashed a cheeky smile. "Is that a promise?"

His mouth reclaimed her mouth, boldly possessed it, and Robyn collapsed against him. Sean wreaked havoc on her body, did things with his lips, tongue and hands that shocked and impressed her. Robyn didn't peg him as the type to share his feelings, but he wasn't afraid to open up to her. He told her how much he desired her and lavished her with compliments. Being with him felt right, as if they were meant to be together, but since Robyn didn't want to scare Sean off, she kept her thoughts to herself.

Seconds passed, then minutes, with no end in sight to the kiss. It was magic, a dream come true. Sean's caresses drove Robyn insane. His hands rode up her thighs, stroked her body with loving tenderness. An amazing sensation flowed through her. Losing herself in the moment, she relished the pleasure of his kiss and the warmth of his touch.

Unable to fight her feelings any longer, she pressed herself against him, her breasts meeting the hard plane of his chest. She wanted more of him, needed more and wasn't afraid to show it. Robyn touched him, stroked his lean physique. She didn't dare hold back. Not now. Not when she desired Sean more than anything and yearned to please him.

Taking the silver bobby pin out of her updo, he buried his hands in her tumbling hair. He cherished her, gave her what she wanted, needed, what her body craved. His tongue probed her mouth, teased and tickled her own, and it took everything in Robyn not to cry out in ecstasy.

Emboldened by his kiss, Robyn gave herself permission to touch the places she'd fantasized about—his nipples, his abs, his butt. Her breathing picked up. The more Robyn stroked Sean, the harder it was to control herself. She was losing it, quickly coming undone, and there was nothing she could do about it. The thrill, the pleasure of stroking his body was the ultimate turn-on.

Sean grabbed her hands and pinned them above her head. As he held them, he lavished her mouth, neck and earlobes with kisses. Pleasure radiated throughout her body, made tingles careen down her spine. He claimed her mouth with his own, made love to it with his skillful tongue. His hot, passionate kiss stole every thought from her mind. Robyn felt as if she was outside herself, off in a different world.

"I've been dreaming about making love to you every night since the last time I was here," he murmured, brushing his mouth against hers. His voice was as smooth as honey; his lips tasted just as sweet. "I hope you've been thinking about me, too."

I have, and I'm so happy you're here I can't wipe this smile off my face.

But she couldn't give voice to the thought. Her mouth wanted to do nothing but kiss Sean.

He didn't wait for her reply. "I feel like a kid in a candy store. There's so much to see and taste and discover." Slipping a hand under her sundress, he caressed her flesh, stroked her nipples through her satin push-up bra until they were erect and throbbing in need. "You feel so damn good."

His touch stole her breath, and Robyn was so turned on by his words she wanted to throw him on the couch, climb onto his lap and ride him until he begged *her* to stop.

"The body never lies." Continuing his sensual assault, he lifted her dress, and placed a finger inside her black thong and stroked her sex. A devilish grin sparked in his eyes and played on his lips. "See, you're wet for me. Wet and eager to please. Right, baby?"

Tremors rocked Robyn's body. Words didn't come. Her eyes rolled to the back of her head, and a moan fell from her lips. She loved what Sean was doing with his hands and prayed he wouldn't stop. His fingers were her undoing; his stroke was what pushed her over the edge. She tumbled into a climax so intense her knees wobbled, and she had to clutch his shoulders so she wouldn't slide to the floor.

Robyn rode his fingers, furiously rocked against them, draining every last second of her orgasm, until finally, she was able to form coherent thought. They'd officially crossed the line, passed the point of no return. This time when Sean undressed her she wouldn't panic, wouldn't ask him to leave. She'd make love to him, would fulfill his every desire. Why not? They liked each other, had amazing chemistry, and if the past few minutes was any indication of what was to come, she was in for one hell of a ride.

The thought made Robyn giddy with excitement. It was high time she did something wild and spontaneous. And why not do it with Sean? Kim and Gabby were out, living it up with their significant others, so it was only fair Robyn have some fun, too. *And I will,* she decided, licking the rim of Sean's ear. *I'm going to do him like he's never been done before.*

Robyn had everything figured out, liked the plan that took shape in her mind. They'd make love, maybe have a shower, and then she'd send Sean on his way, because if Kim saw him leaving her suite tomorrow morning, there'd be hell to pay. Robyn didn't want to end up at the unemployment office. The Belleza Resort had no rival, no equal, and she was proud to be the lead event planner of the number-one resort in California.

Sean smiled, and it dazzled her. "Bringing you dinner tonight was the smartest thing I've ever done."

"I don't want to hurt Kim or your parents," Robyn said, fighting to catch her breath. "They can never, ever find out about this."

"I don't want to talk about them. I want to talk about you."

Sean slid a second finger inside her panties and smiled triumphantly when another moan fell from her lips. Robyn knew she should pull away, knew that was the right thing to do, but she didn't have the willpower it required. She wanted him, craved him in ways even she didn't understand, and she was determined to have him. He seemed to take great pleasure in pleasing her, and whispered sweet words in her ears.

Like firecrackers, pleasure exploded inside her body, and several seconds passed before her breathing slowed. It took supreme effort, everything she had not to rip Sean's clothes from his body and ride him until the break of dawn. Robyn hadn't been intimate with a man in years, and she relished the pleasure of being in his arms.

"What's your fantasy?" Sean asked her, breaking into her thoughts.

You mean, besides making love to you all over my apartment?

Robyn licked her lips, then drew a deep breath. It was hard to concentrate with Sean's fingers between her legs, hard to think about anything but how good he was making her feel. She struggled to find the words. "I—I don't know," she stammered. "I've never given it much thought."

"Of course you have. Everyone does." He stared deep into her eyes as if he was trying to reach her hidden thoughts, then leaned forward until their heads were touching. "It's nothing to be ashamed of, Robyn. Fantasies are a sign of a healthy imagination, and since you're the most creative person I know, I bet your fantasies are epic."

"No, not really. They're pretty typical—" Robyn broke off speaking, but it was too late to cram the words back into her mouth.

Sean looked proud, as if he'd just hit a home run, and spoke in a deep, husky tone of voice. "Now we're getting somewhere," he said with a grin. "Tell me."

Her lips were dry, her throat, too, but she told him the truth, something she'd only shared with her friends over cocktails. "I've always fantasized about having sex in a luxury car."

"I have several. Take your pick."

The twinkle in his eye and the mischievous expression on his face was a turn-on. She wasn't aggressive by nature, but her desire for Sean was so powerful she ripped off his shirt, pushed it over his shoulders and stroked his lean, ripped torso.

"Anywhere else?"

"A swimming pool."

"I have one." His smile widened. "We'll have to make your fantasies a reality soon."

You won't get any protests out of me!

"Do you have any idea what you're doing to me right now?" Sean took her hand and placed it on his erection. "Do you feel that? How hard I am for you?"

Robyn was silent for a moment, as still as a mannequin. She didn't know what to say and feared she'd trip over her tongue if she spoke. Her heart belonged to Sean, her body, too, and she'd do anything to please him, even step out of her comfort zone.

Robyn heard her cell phone ringing, but she ignored it. Being with Sean was all that mattered, and she didn't want anything to ruin the mood. Cupping his face in her hands, she kissed him deeply with all the hunger and passion thrumming in her veins. He made her feel desirable in a way she'd never felt before, and Robyn sensed it was going to be a night she'd never forget.

A heady scent swirled around the room, like a sweet, fragrant mist, and the air was charged with desire. Pressing her mouth to his skin, she kissed his flesh from his neck to his chest and back again. Hearing his groans boosted her confidence, gave Robyn the encouragement she needed to take the next step.

Eager to please, she knelt before him and unbuttoned his shorts with her teeth.

"Damn, where did you learn to do that?"

Robyn wore an innocent face. *"The Kama Sutra."*

"Do you know any other tricks?"

"If you play your cards right I might show you a thing or two."

Tossing aside his shorts, she freed his erection from his black boxer briefs. Her mouth watered at the sight of his package. It was long and thick, standing at attention to greet her. Robyn tasted him with the tip of her tongue, flicked it playfully against him.

Robyn licked his erection as if it was a chocolate ice-cream cone. She gripped his butt to keep him right where she wanted him and swirled her tongue around his length. She raised her gaze to find Sean watching her with admiration in his eyes. Knowing that she was pleasing him made Robyn feel proud.

Nipping at his package with her teeth, she used her hands to massage his body. Robyn took him deeper into her mouth, and she felt strong, empowered, like a badass chick at the top of her game.

Sean buried his hands in her hair. He groaned her name over and over again as his body shuddered. Excited, Robyn sucked him harder, faster. Sean was losing his cool, unraveling right before her eyes, and she got a kick out of watching her strong, virile lover lose control.

Then, with his hand on her shoulders, he pulled her up to her feet. Why was he stopping her? She wanted to give him the pleasure he'd given her before. But she could form no protest as he smothered her lips with his own. He held her in his hands, caressed her like a potter molding clay. "Let's go to bed," he whispered against her mouth.

Desperate for him, she took his hands. "Right this way, sexy."

But having been to her condo before, Sean knew where the master bedroom was and led her down the darkened hallway, kissing her every step of the way.

Entering the bedroom, he flipped on the lights with one hand and closed the door with the back of his foot.

In no time their clothes were removed and thrown to the ground, littering the plush, beige carpet.

He lovingly massaged her breasts, kissed each erect nipple. Robyn cried out, clung to him for fear of losing control. She had an insatiable thirst for Sean and couldn't get enough of his touch, his kiss. "I don't know about you," he murmured, sliding his hands over her butt and giving it a hard squeeze. "But I'm ready for the main event."

Laughing, their hands intertwined, Sean and Robyn collapsed onto the bed.

Sean had never seen a more beautiful woman. He marveled at Robyn's curvy, figure. Her perky nipples, her hips, her toned legs, which went on for miles. The sight of her naked body caused his erection to rise. Showing up at her condo had been a calculated risk, but he'd never been one to play by the rules and refused to let his family keep them apart. Not when they clicked on every level—especially in the bedroom.

Hungry for her, he tipped his head toward her and kissed her hard on the lips. She had a tight little ass he loved rubbing and stroking and squeezing. Sean couldn't get enough of her. Couldn't stop kissing her, playing in her hair, telling her how gorgeous she was, how sexy. She was his fantasy, and her pleasure was his only concern.

He spread her legs wide open. So wide, he couldn't resist burying his face there for a taste. He'd never given a woman oral sex before, but it was different with Robyn. He wanted to please her, to prove he was the only man she'd ever need. To do that, he planned to make her come over and over again.

Sean licked her inner thighs, showered kisses along

her warm, soft flesh. Gripping her hips, he slid his tongue back and forth across her clit. The payoff was immediate. Robyn clutched his head in her hands and rocked her hips. She spread her legs wider, invited him in to explore her body. It was a sexy, erotic moment, one Sean would never forget.

Bursting with confidence, he put his tongue to work. He flicked it against her sweet spot, teased and tickled it until she cried out. Planting her feet on the bed, she gripped the headboard, used it as leverage to match him thrust for thrust. He sucked her lips into his mouth, and her moans grew stronger, louder, until they filled the room. Sean glanced up at Robyn just in time to see her orgasm hit and a look of pure bliss cover her face.

"Do you have condoms?"

Robyn looked sleepy, but she rolled onto her side and gestured to the mahogany table.

Sean opened the drawer, found a box, took a packet out and ripped it open. He rolled on the condom, rejoined Robyn in bed and gathered her in his arms. Raining kisses across her face, he stroked her body with his hands.

Robyn seized his erection, parted her legs and guided him inside her treasure. His length filled her, possessed her. She felt incredible, tighter than tight, even better than he'd imagined. They moved as one, slowly at first, then picked up speed as her muscles relaxed.

Sweat clung to his skin, and his temperature climbed higher with each thrust. No one wanted a robot in bed, and not only did Robyn meet his intensity, she unleashed her inner vixen. Their lovemaking was primal, explosive, without a doubt the most erotic experience of his life. It was important to him, imperative even, that sex was enjoyable for her, the best she'd ever had. He wanted to be the only man in her life, the person she confided in, but more than anything he wanted her love. He had no one on his side and valued having Robyn in his corner. She was the kind of woman he could see himself settling down with, and he wanted her for more than just one night. Forever.

Sean held her close to his chest, nipped and tickled her earlobe with his tongue. She giggled, and the sound brought a proud smile to his mouth. There was nothing better than making love to her. Her moans made him feel like a superstar. Watching her come undone, feeling her body quiver and shudder beneath his, was the greatest thrill.

Wanting to make the most of their time together, Sean cautioned himself to relax, to take his time. But it was too late. Tingles tickled the tips of his ears, then shot to his toes. He was burning up, and his skin felt hotter than a flame. Sean pressed his eyes shut, tried to control his body, but he lost the battle with his flesh. He was coming, losing it, and hoped he wouldn't embarrass himself when his orgasm finally hit.

Spasms filled with electric currents pulsed through his groin, stealing his breath. They were so powerful, so crippling and intense Sean feared he'd black out. As he climaxed, every muscle in his body tensed and contracted.

Satisfied but exhausted, Sean collapsed onto the bed and released a deep, ragged breath. Robyn rested her head on his chest. Stroking her hair, neck and shoulders, he told her how special she was, how much she mattered to him, that she was the only woman he desired. Robyn listened, didn't speak, but he sensed that she was pleased.

Sleep made his eyes heavy and his limbs weak. Worried he was going to doze off, Sean sat up, swung his legs over the side of the canopy bed and searched for his clothes.

"You're leaving?"

Sean heard the quiver in her voice, saw the uncertainty in the depths of her eyes and shook his head. "No way. You can't get rid of me that easily." He tipped his head toward her and kissed the tip of her nose. "I just need something to drink. Can I get you anything?"

"You sound like a waiter."

"A good chef does it all, and I pride myself on being hands-on in and *out* of the kitchen."

Sean expected Robyn to laugh, but she didn't. A pensive expression covered her face, and panic filled him with dread. Did she regret making love to him? Was she having second thoughts about him spending the night? A lump formed in his throat. Was she unsatisfied?

He studied her, tried to make sense of her furrowed brow. Robyn looked as if she wanted to say something, but didn't, and since Sean didn't want to question her for fear of looking clingy, he swiped his boxer briefs off the floor and put them on. "Are you sure I can't get you anything from the kitchen?"

"I'd love another glass of chardonnay, if you don't mind."

"I don't mind at all. One glass of chardonnay, coming right up."

"On second thought, just bring the bottle."

"You're a lush." Sean flashed a grin. "Sexy as hell, but definitely a lush."

A pillow hit the wall, narrowly missing his head, and Sean chuckled. He enjoyed joking around with Robyn, liked that she didn't take life too seriously or get bent out of shape when he teased her. Heading for the kitchen, he made a mental note to bring her something to eat, as well.

Sean stopped short, couldn't believe what he saw. Chairs were overturned in the living room, the furniture was out of place and they must have accidently knocked Robyn's purse over in their haste to get to the bedroom because its contents were strewn all over the floor.

Bending down, Sean retrieved everything from under the breakfast bar and shoved it back inside her tote bag. Picking up her leather planner, he was surprised to see the note she'd written on an upcoming date: *Lunch with Enrique Salazar at The Pearl.*

Confused, Sean scratched his head. Robyn had written two paragraphs about the Mexican billionaire, and as he read her detailed notes, his spirits sank. The business magnate was a brown-eyed charmer who collected beautiful women like trophies, and unfortunately, Robyn was exactly his type—tall, curvy, feisty. Enrique's father, Mauricio, was a close friend of Sean's dad, and over the years, the two families had become close. But that didn't mean he was going to stand by and let Enrique steal his girl. Sean was bound and determined to take Robyn off the market and couldn't risk her falling under the tycoon's spell. Not when they were finally making progress.

Sean raked a hand over his head, tried to formulate a plan to keep his girl and his friend apart. He hadn't spoken to Enrique in months, not since he'd left the resort and moved to LA. Had no desire to. Losing the Belleza to Kim was not only a crushing blow but a personal embarrassment, one he didn't feel comfortable talking about to anyone except Robyn.

He stood up. His thoughts raced. Why was Robyn having lunch with Enrique? How did she know him? Had

Kim set them up? Something Robyn had said earlier, while they were having dinner, replayed in his mind, intensifying his fears. His sister had always loved playing matchmaker, but according to Robyn, Kim was desperate to set her up with one of her fiancé's single, successful friends. *Yeah, over my dead body,* he vowed, stalking over to the stainless-steel fridge and yanking open the door. There was no way in hell he'd stand by and watch Robyn date other men.

Sean wanted to ask Robyn about her lunch date, but he didn't want to ruin their romantic night. She'd accuse him of snooping and probably kick him out of her condo, and Sean wasn't ready for their time together to end. Going home to his empty house held no appeal, neither did getting into an argument with Robyn about her personal life. To get to the bottom of things, he'd touch base with Enrique and find out exactly what was going on. But not tonight.

Sniffing the air, he smelled incense burning, and wondered if his lady love was reading his mind. Grabbing everything he needed, Sean closed the fridge and turned off the lights in the kitchen. Whistling a tune, he strode back down the hallway.

Entering the bedroom, Sean was pleasantly surprised to find Robyn sitting up in bed, singing the song playing on the stereo, rocking her body from side to side.

"Took you long enough," she quipped with a laugh. "I was just about to come get you."

"Be patient, baby girl. Good things come to those who wait."

"What's all that?"

"Dessert." Sean knew he looked a sight, holding a wine bottle in one hand, and strawberries, chocolate syrup and vanilla ice cream in the other. He flashed a boyish smile. "Ready for round two?"

Her eyes sparkled, and a smirk filled her lips. "You don't even have to ask."

Chapter 8

Robyn woke up on Thursday morning to the sound of twittering birds outside her bedroom window. Chilled, she closed her eyes and snuggled deeper into the satin sheets. Robyn had a full day ahead of her, but she gave herself permission to relax in bed for a few more minutes. Her brain felt foggy, her legs were sore, and her body ached all over. That was no surprise. She'd had sex with Sean—not once, not twice, but three mind-blowing times. And had it ever felt good.

Wild. Passionate. Exhilarating. Like a real-life episode of *Sex in the City*.

Memories of their sensuous encounter warmed Robyn all over. X-rated images scrolled through her mind, and each picture was more erotic than the last. Sean was a patient, considerate lover, playful and frisky in bed, too. Laughing and joking around with him made Robyn feel less self-conscious about her body, more confident and secure, and when she'd dozed off in the wee hours of the morning, it had been with a dreamy smile on her face.

Wanting to hear Sean's voice—to prove their connection was real and not something she'd imagined—Robyn rolled onto her side and grabbed the cordless phone off the bedside table. She punched in his number and waited anxiously for the call to connect. Like her, Sean was an early riser who woke up every morning raring and ready to go. He was probably already at the SP Grill, hard at work in the kitchen, so she'd have to keep their conversation brief.

Robyn heard music playing inside her en suite bathroom and instantly recognized the catchy Drake song as Sean's ring tone. Confused, she hung up the phone. Had Sean forgotten his cell? Did he know it was missing? Tossing her blanket aside, Robyn jumped to her feet and rushed into the bathroom.

And there, sitting on the counter, was Sean's cell phone.

Hearing a noise, her eyes narrowed and her ears perked up. Had she left the TV on last night? Was housekeeping doing their weekly cleaning? Creaking open the bedroom door, she peered out into the hallway, listened for a minute. Someone was in the kitchen—opening cupboards, rifling through the pantry, fiddling with the stereo—and Robyn knew who it was. Her heart was beating so loud she couldn't hear herself think, and her stomach was coiled into a knot. *No! No! No! It can't be!*

Panic slammed into her chest, stealing her breath. Her pulse roared in her ears, sounded like an out-of-control freight train zipping down the tracks, and her hands began to sweat and shake. Robyn had a vague recollection of Sean kissing her goodbye, so hearing him in her kitchen, humming to the Jodeci song playing on the radio, puzzled her.

Questions overran her mind, questions she didn't have answers to. Why was Sean still here? Didn't he understand the risks, what was at stake? Was he trying to get her fired?

Desperate to get to the bottom of things, Robyn threw open her bedroom door and charged down the hallway. As she passed a mirror hanging on the wall, she caught a glimpse of herself and stopped abruptly.

Good God, she thought, staring at her reflection. *I could scare Frankenstein.* Her hair was standing on end, and her pink satin nightie was a wrinkled mess. Not a good look. Before she saw Sean, a shower and a wardrobe change were definitely in order.

Spinning back around, she returned to the bedroom and grabbed everything she needed to make herself look more presentable. Robyn heard her cell phone chime, signaling she had a new text message, and glanced around the room in search of it.

Robyn spotted it on the dresser, picked it up and typed in her password. She had three missed calls and dozens of text messages. She already knew she was in trouble with her mom for not getting in touch last night. Her mother had retired from nursing last year, sold her condo and moved to Palm Springs. Robyn loved having her mom nearby and made time to see her a few times a month. She wanted to phone her mom to touch base, but first she had to sort things out with Sean.

After a quick shower, Robyn put on a turquoise halter-neck sundress, which accentuated her shape. Diamond stud earrings and bejeweled sandals complimented her easy, breezy look. She wanted to curl her hair and do her makeup, but there was no time. She had to send Sean on his way before someone discovered he was at the resort and ratted her out to Kim. Or worse, called the police.

Robyn banished the thought. *Don't go there. It's not going to happen. Your secret's safe.*

Feeling more confident about facing her one-night stand, despite the butterflies in her stomach, she headed for the kitchen. The blinds were drawn, and the balcony doors were wide open. Warmth and sunshine flooded the living room. A fruity aroma was heavy in the air, and Robyn's mouth watered at the scent of fresh fruit.

Her feet slowed to a stop, and goose bumps prickled her skin. *Whoa, baby!* There was nothing better than finding a half-naked man in the kitchen, making breakfast. Robyn stared at Sean with longing, admired his strong, athletic physique. Seeing Sean at the stove, flipping pancakes, made Robyn hungry for more than just food. Her hands itched to touch him, to stroke him all over, but she was determined to keep her wits about her.

Robyn was surprised to see that the breakfast bar was covered with a delicious array of foods. Eggs Benedict, bacon casserole, chocolate-chip waffles topped with whipped cream, maple syrup and strawberries. If not for the dirty dishes piled high in the sink, she would've thought it was room service, but it was obvious Sean had cooked everything himself. The food was a feast for the eyes and so was her drop-dead sexy chef with the tight butt.

"See something you like?"

Do. I. Ever. Robyn tried to speak, but her lips wouldn't work. Her body did, though. Her nipples hardened, her sex was tingling uncontrollably, and desire roared through her veins. *What's the matter with me? Why am I acting like this? It was just one night.*

Embarrassed that Sean had caught her staring at him, she raised her head from his muscular body and met his gaze. His boyish smile—the warmth and tenderness of it—made Robyn's heart leap inside her chest, and the urge to kiss him was so overwhelming it dominated her thoughts.

"Good morning," Robyn said quietly, wishing her limbs would quit shaking. Last night in bed, she'd talked dirty and done things she'd never done before, but in the light of day, she had zero confidence.

"Good morning, yourself." Sean must have sensed her anxiety, her inner turmoil, because he turned off the stove and took her in his arms. "You're looking gorgeous, as usual."

"Thanks. Did you sleep well?" she asked, determined to conquer her nerves.

His smile widened, lit up his entire face. "Of course I did. I spent the night with the woman of my dreams."

Robyn wasn't sure if Sean was speaking from the heart or just feeding her a well-rehearsed line, so she asked the question weighing heavily on her mind. "I'm surprised you're still here. Aren't you supposed to be at the restaurant?"

"You don't remember, do you?"

"Remember what?"

"Cornering me in the bathroom and having your way with me."

Heat burned her cheeks. The air was electric, charged with fire and desire. It was a fight, a struggle to stay in the moment when all Robyn wanted to do was make love again. She had an aching need for him, a hunger that threatened to consume her, and his deadly sexy gaze only fanned the flames.

"You can be quite persuasive, Ms. Henderson." He lowered his lips to her ear, spoke in a husky bravado that spoke of his insatiable need. "And when you dropped to your knees and took me in your mouth, that sealed the deal."

He kissed her then, boldly claimed her mouth with his own. Robyn suspected Sean was trying to jog her memory with his lips; he didn't, but she appreciated his effort. She loved kissing him, could never get enough of him and wished she didn't have to kick him out. But she did. And she had to do it now, before things spiraled out of control.

Too late. His lips were everywhere, his hands, too. Playing with her hair, fondling her breasts, stroking her hips, grabbing her behind as if it belonged to him. Groaning, as if in physical torment, he ground himself against her, boldly rubbed his erection back and forth against her sex. The move made Robyn's brain turn to mush and her body quiver like jelly.

Abandoning herself to his kiss, Robyn pressed her chest against his and curled her arms around his waist. She wished they could spend the rest of the day in bed, but they couldn't, she thought sadly, touching his face. *One last kiss and then I'm sending you on your way.*

Robyn broke off the kiss, but Sean held her tighter, refused to let her go.

"Do you want dessert now or after breakfast?" he asked, nibbling on her earlobe.

"Wow, that's some spread. You made enough food to feed the Belleza staff."

"You deserve it. You worked up quite an appetite last

night, and besides, I love cooking for you." A grin played on his lips. "You can repay me in kisses. Go ahead. Lay one on me."

"I'd love to." Robyn leaned forward, gave him a peck on the cheek and giggled when he poked out his bottom lip. He affectionately squeezed her hips, and she secretly wished his hands would travel south. *Way* down south. To the treasure between her legs. She wanted him, craved him like a cold drink on a scorching, hot day, but she didn't have the guts to make the first move. At least not in the kitchen. In the bedroom, after dark, was another story.

"That's all I get for slaving over a hot stove? One measly peck on the cheek?"

"Yup!" Wearing a mischievous smile, Robyn plucked a mini cinnamon roll out of the glass bowl and popped it into her mouth. It was sweet and moist, and within seconds, she'd polished off another one. "I'd better stop. I have a bridesmaid dress to fit into next month, and I don't want to look like a beached whale on Kim's big day."

His face stiffened, and his lips twisted in distaste. "My sister doesn't deserve your devotion. She doesn't know anything about loyalty or a damn thing about love."

"Sean, that's not fair."

"Yes, it is." Anger covered his face, radiated off him in waves. "You don't know Kim the way I do. She's always had my dad wrapped around her little finger."

"And *you've* always been the apple of your mother's eye."

"That's not the point."

"Then help me understand, because I still don't get why you're mad at Kim. What did she do that was so wrong? It was your parents' decision to award her control of the resort."

He flinched as if he'd been sucker punched, but Robyn didn't hold back. Not this time. She was determined to speak her mind. Had to. No matter what. This conversation was long overdue; she should have set Sean straight the night he showed up on her doorstep months ago instead of making out with him. It was imperative she tell him the truth. Not for Kim's sake, but for his own, before he lost his family for good. "What did you expect Kim to do? Turn down the job she's wanted her whole life?"

"That's what I would have done."

"You're lying," she argued, not believing him for a second. "You know good and well if your dad had awarded you control of the Belleza you would have taken the job in a heartbeat."

Robyn expected Sean to argue, but he remained silent. Desperate to get through to him, she spoke from the heart. "Kim feels you abandoned her, and my heart breaks for her because unfortunately I know exactly what she's going through. I've been there, and it's a horrible feeling to have someone you love turn their back on you."

He stared at her, didn't say a word, and she could tell by the pensive expression on his face, by the sadness that flickered in his eyes that her words had hit home. Robyn was hopeful she'd gotten through to him, but what he said next left her speechless.

"I hope my issues with Kim aren't going to affect our relationship, because I need you in my life, and I'm willing to do anything to make us work."

Robyn wished he would stop saying things like that. Her heart couldn't take it.

Suddenly thirsty, she picked up the water jug, filled her glass and took a long drink.

"I knew there was something special about you the moment we met, and last night confirmed it," he continued in a silky soft tone. "We were meant to be."

Her mind was reeling, spinning out-of-control, and her heart was beating in double-time. She was dreaming, right? Had to be. This wasn't Sean. He didn't do relationships, was deathly afraid of commitment and had a reputation for being a ruthless heartbreaker. And Robyn didn't want to be the next casualty on his hit list. A night of wild, passionate sex was one thing; riding off into the sunset with her best friend's estranged brother was another issue altogether.

"I want us to date exclusively from here on out."

Robyn fervently shook her head. "I don't have time to date."

"Make time. I want to wine you and dine you and show you off at black-tie events—"

"Sean, you're getting way ahead of yourself. It was just one night."

"This isn't about sex."

Of course it is, she thought. *What else could it be about?*

Hearing the wall clock chime, Robyn glanced over her shoulder and checked the time. It was eight o'clock on the dot. Sighing in relief, she felt tension and anxiety leave her body. By now, most—if not all—of the resort staff were at work, so the chance of someone seeing Sean leave her condo was slim to none. But to be on the safe side, she'd lend him a hat, a hoodie and a pair of dark sunglasses. Better safe than sorry, *because if Kim finds out I slept with Sean I can kiss our friendship goodbye.*

"You're the right woman for me, the *only* woman for me…" Trailing off, he cupped her chin in his hand and kissed her slowly, thoughtfully on the lips. His grip was tight around her waist, possessive, and his tongue danced inside her mouth, arousing every cell in her body. "And," he said, trailing a finger along her bare shoulder, "I want to make you come every single night, over and over and over again."

How she loved the sound of that. But she was scared to death his family would find out about them.

"Promise me you'll give some serious thought to what I said."

Robyn nodded. "I promise. Now can we eat? I'm so hungry I'm dizzy."

Sean flashed a broad, sexy grin. "I've been told I have that effect on women."

"You wish! I swear, if your ego was any bigger you wouldn't be able to fit your head through the door!"

He gave a hearty laugh, and the sound warmed Robyn all over.

"Let's eat on the patio. It's a hot, sunny day."

"I'm fine right here." Robyn grabbed a plate, piled it high with her favorite foods and plopped down on a stool. No way could they eat outside where people could see them. "Besides, I like to watch the morning news while I eat breakfast."

Sean picked up the remote, turned on the TV and sat down beside her. He kept a hand draped behind her chair and stroked her neck and shoulders as she ate. Damn, did it ever feel good, but it was distracting, and she struggled to focus on what he was saying. He had the whole day planned for them, and his enthusiasm was so palpable, so contagious she wanted to kiss him for being so thoughtful and sweet.

Giddy with excitement, Robyn could hardly sit still. Sean was in a class all his own and the most amazing lover she'd ever had. Too bad he was at odds with Kim.

Someone knocked on the door, and Robyn almost jumped out of her skin. Her fork slipped from her hand and fell to her plate. Had Sean been outside on the patio? Did someone call Kim? Or worse, the Belleza police? Would he be arrested for trespassing?

"Are you expecting someone?"

Breaking free of her thoughts, she shook her head and swallowed the food in her mouth.

"No worries," Sean said, tossing his napkin on his empty plate. "I'll get rid of them."

"Oh, no, you don't." To prevent him from going into the foyer, Robyn slid in front of him and pointed down the hallway. "You're going to go get dressed, and you're going to do it now."

"I love when you boss me around. It's such a turn-on." Sean stalked out of the kitchen, and Robyn watched his every move. He moved with confidence, like a man who was used to having his way, and his walk was as captivating as his smile. Memories of them making love consumed her thoughts, arousing her afresh.

A loud noise yanked Robyn out of her thoughts. In the foyer, she cracked open the front door. Kim and Gabby were standing in the hallway, wearing matching frowns. Sweat broke out on her skin, and her temperature spiked. What were they doing here? Did they know Sean was inside her suite?

"How come you were a no-show at Pilates?" Gabby asked, raising an eyebrow.

"I, uh, slept in." To prevent them from coming inside, Robyn stepped into the hallway and closed the door behind her. Kim and Gabby exchanged a puzzled look, but she pretended not to notice. Fresh faced and pretty in tank tops and shorts, her friends could easily be mistaken for college students on summer vacation. "How was class?"

"Boring without you."

Lowering her gaze to the floor, Robyn fiddled with her silver charm bracelet on her left arm. Robyn couldn't look Kim in the eye, not after all the salacious things she'd done with Sean last night in bed. She struggled to speak.

"Do you have any pancakes left?" Kim asked, wetting her lips with her tongue.

Robyn frowned and cocked her head to the right. "How do you know I made breakfast?"

"Because I can smell your yummy cooking all the way outside." Kim groaned and rubbed her stomach as if she was dying of hunger. "I'm starving."

"Now is, uh, not a good time."

"Of course it is. You're working from home. You have all the time in the world."

"Actually, I was just leaving. I have some, uh, running around to do."

"I have to go, too." Gabby raised her cell phone in the air. "I just got a text from Charlene. She's home sick in bed, which means I'll have to do double duty at the restaurant."

"Well, be careful, because the last time you filled in for one of your staff, you got a lot more than you bargained for," Robyn warned, giving her friend a knowing smile. Gabby had met her fiancé, Geoffrey Girard, at The Pearl last month, while waiting tables, and like Kim and Jaxon, they'd been inseparable from the moment they'd met. "Guys go gaga over you, so just make sure you're not *too* friendly with the male patrons."

Love twinkled in her eyes, and a dreamy expression covered her face. "Geoffrey is the only man I need, and no one else can ever take his place."

I feel the exact same way about Sean.

"Maybe we can do dinner tonight," Kim proposed. "Jaxon took me to a Colombian restaurant a couple months ago, and I want to visit it again. I know you guys will love it."

"I can't. I'm going to Posh Lounge tonight."

"Really? With who? Your mom?"

Robyn laughed, not because the question was absurd, but because her best friend knew her so well. She often went with her mom on her days off, especially now that Kim and Gabby were always off doing something with their fiancés. "Yeah," she said nonchalantly, hoping and praying Sean wasn't on the other side of the door, listening to her lie through her teeth. "I'd better get going. I have a million and one things to do today."

"Have fun tonight," Gabby said. "And give your mom my regards."

"Me, too, and don't forget to invite her to my Jack and Jill bridal shower."

Guilt tormented her conscience, made it impossible for Robyn to return Kim's smile. She'd given her best friend a hard time for hooking up with Jaxon Dunham back in June, but she'd done much worse last night. Not only had she slept with Sean, she'd told him about all of the problems at the resort, knowing full well the police considered him a suspect.

"See you guys later. I'll text you." Waving, Robyn watched as her friends headed toward their respective residences. She slipped back inside her condo, collapsed against the door and released the breath she'd been holding for the last five minutes. That was a close one, she thought, mopping the sweat from her brow. But she wasn't out of the woods just yet. She still had to smuggle Sean out of her condo.

Chapter 9

"Cute car," Robyn said, struggling to keep a straight face. "It's *totally* you!"

"Ha-ha, very funny." Sean was driving west on the I-10, toward Los Angeles, and she'd been teasing him about his smart car for the last ten minutes. It felt good to laugh, especially after the morning she'd had. Sneaking Sean out of her condo had been stressful, but after several close calls with housekeeping, they'd made it to his car and sped out of the parking lot like a pair of bandits. "If Ryan could see you now, he'd probably die laughing."

"No, he'd kick my ass for tarnishing the Parker image." Sean chuckled good-naturedly, then shrugged his shoulders. "I knew my Bugatti would attract unwanted attention at the resort, so I switched cars with my assistant manager. Needless to say Jolene was thrilled."

"You let your assistant drive your sports car? Wow, you guys must be close."

"I'm not sleeping with her, if that's what you're implying."

Good, because I don't want to share you with anyone else.

"Isn't it obvious how I feel about you?" He met her gaze. "I'm serious about you, Robyn. That's why I came to the resort last night."

Studying his profile, she noted his calm disposition, how relaxed and at ease he looked behind the wheel of the car. His hair and mustache were neatly trimmed, but the stubble along his jaw gave him a rugged edge, one she was wholly attracted to.

"Coming to the resort was risky. What if security had seen you and called the cops? Or tried to apprehend you themselves?"

"The thought never crossed my mind. I was bound and determined to see you last night, and I wasn't going to let anything stop me." Sean reached across the center console and placed a hand on her thigh. His tone, the intensity of his gaze and his soothing touch made her heart flutter inside her chest. "You're important to me, Robyn, and I'll do anything for you."

To that, Robyn didn't know what to say. To fill the silence she asked Sean about the SP Grill. "On Monday at lunch, you mentioned your issues with the construction company," she said, recalling their conversation during dessert. "Has everything finally been resolved?"

"Yes, thankfully, and once the building inspection is completed next week the SP Grill should get its certificate of occupancy." He spoke openly about the pressure he was under, about his burning desire to succeed in the restaurant business, and Robyn assured him he would.

As they drove, they discussed the LA food-and-wine festival and the upcoming Usher concert.

"Are you hungry?" Sean asked, glancing at her.

Robyn shook her head. "I'm still full from breakfast."

"Cool. Then let's head straight to the beach." Parting his lips, he moistened them with his tongue. "I hope you packed your bathing suit, because we're going to spend the rest of the morning in the water."

"I'm wearing my bikini under my sundress."

His ardent gaze slid down her body, and Robyn wished his hands would follow suit.

"Smart and sexy. I like."

I like you, too. More than I've ever liked anyone.

Who are you kidding? questioned her inner voice. *You passed* like *a long time ago.*

"Let's swim first. It's a weekday, so we'll probably have the beach to ourselves."

His cell phone rang, and he fished it out of his shirt pocket. Sean pressed the speaker button, and said, "Hey, Jolene, what's up? I hope you're taking good care of my baby."

"Likewise. Bring my car back in one piece."

"How are things going at the restaurant?"

"Good," she replied, her tone bright and sunny. "But I wish you were here."

Robyn listened closely for several minutes and decided Sean's assistant manager definitely had a crush on him. The woman giggled every few minutes, was blatantly flirting with him, and Robyn just knew she was smiling from ear-to-ear on the other end of the line.

"Are you going to be in soon?"

Sean winked at Robyn but addressed his assistant.

"No, not today. I'm taking a personal day, but if you need me you can reach me on my cell."

"What am I supposed to tell your mom?" she asked, her tone filled with concern. "She's been here for almost an hour, and she's growing impatient waiting for you."

"My mom's there?"

Robyn felt her mouth dry and her heart race. What was Mrs. Parker doing at the SP Grill? Was Mr. Parker with her? A cold, shiver whipped through her body, and panic drenched her skin. Had they discovered Sean had spent the night at her condo? Were they planning to fire her when she returned to the resort? Robyn couldn't breathe, struggled to catch her breath. She had a million questions for his assistant manager but remained quiet. It was none of her business, and since she didn't want Sean to get mad at her for butting in, she took her cell phone out of her purse and checked her email. She had dozens of new work messages but struggled to concentrate on what she was reading.

"Your mom was waiting in the parking lot when I arrived this morning, so I let her in. Do you want to speak to her?"

Sean didn't answer, and Robyn nudged him in the ribs with her elbow. "Yes," she mouthed. "It's your mom. You *have* to talk to her."

Mrs. Parker's voice floated over the phone line, and Robyn couldn't help but smile. The mother of three was a smart, spunky woman who loved life, and Robyn enjoyed spending time with her. Mr. Parker? Not so much. He was serious and curt, and the only time he looked happy was when he was with Kimberly, his one and only daughter.

"Hello, Mom," Sean said. "I wish you would have called before driving all the way out to LA."

"I've been calling you practically every day for the last eight months," she argued.

"I've been busy."

"Too busy to call your own mother?"

"No, Mom, of course not." Sean raked a hand over his head, and expelled a deep breath. "I just needed some time away to clear my head."

"I miss you, Sean. Things just aren't the same without you. Please come back to Belleza. You belong with your family."

Mrs. Parker's voice cracked with emotion, and hearing her bitter anguish broke Robyn's heart. Tears blurred her vision, and it took everything she had not to cry. "Go to the restaurant and speak to your mom," she whispered, turning to him. "It's the right thing to do."

Sean shook his head. "I can't."

"Please? For me?" she begged, desperate to get through to him. "Your mom needs you."

Picking up his cell phone, he put it to his ear and spoke in a soft, soothing voice. It was obvious Sean loved his mom, and Robyn knew the feeling was mutual. Every time she ran into the Parkers at the resort, Ilene made a point of mentioning everything Sean had done to make The Pearl the success it was. People came from far and wide to dine at the award-winning restaurant, and Robyn didn't blame them. The ambiance was perfect, the food delicious. Gabby had definitely picked up where Sean had left off.

"Mom, don't cry. I'll call you tomorrow, okay?" He paused, scratched at the stubble on his jaw. "I love you, too. Drive home safe."

Seconds later, Sean ended the call and dropped his cell phone into the cup holder. He stared aimlessly out the windshield, and Robyn could tell by the expression on his face that the conversation with his mom had shaken him up. His eyes were sad, frown lines wrinkled his forehead, and he seemed to be lost in another world.

Silence followed, and the air inside the car grew thick. Robyn rolled down the passenger-side window and breathed deeply through her nose. It didn't help. She felt horrible, as if she was to blame for Sean not going to the restaurant to see his mom, and wanted to rectify the situation. But how? They drove in silence, and although it felt like an eternity, Robyn knew she had to give Sean his space. Asking questions would only make him feel worse, and she didn't want to say anything to hurt his feelings. Sean talked big, especially about not needing his family, but deep down, he was a softie who craved his father's acceptance, and that would never change.

"You must think I'm a jerk for the way I treated my mom."

"No, I don't," she said. "It's obvious you love her, and that's all that matters."

Sean exited the freeway, and after driving another ten miles, turned into the Manhattan Beach parking lot. He shut off the car, and Robyn knew it was her chance to do the right thing. What she should have done earlier. "I can take a cab home so you can go to the restaurant and see your mom."

"Robyn, don't tell me what to do."

"Someone has to. You're not thinking clearly, and you're hurting the people you love."

"Why do you care what happens in my family? What's it to you?"

"This isn't about me. This is about you doing the right thing, and that's reconciling with your family." Robyn didn't want to argue with Sean—not after the magical night they'd shared—but he needed to hear the truth, and she wasn't letting him off the hook this time. "Running from your problems isn't helping. If anything, it's making the situation worse. Go home, sit down with your parents and work things out."

Sean released a deep sigh. He looked drained, as if he'd just finished a grueling workout, nothing like his confident, self-assured self. "Not today," he said, shaking his head. "I don't want to talk about Kim or the resort or what a disappointment I am to my family, either."

His words shocked her. "What are you talking about?" Reaching out, she touched a hand to his cheek, forcing him to look at her. When he did, she smiled at him, tried to communicate what was in her heart through her eyes. "Sean, don't talk like that. You're a brilliant, acclaimed chef who's about to take the restaurant world by storm. It's just a matter of time before you knock Wolfgang Puck off his throne!"

"You're just saying that because I made you breakfast."

"No, it's the truth." To make him smile, Robyn pressed her lips to his ear and spoke in a sultry voice. "And you're a world-class lover, too. Every time I think about last night, I get wet."

A sly grin warmed his expression. Robyn leaned into him, pressed her mouth to his. She couldn't help it. She had to do it. She wanted to erase the sadness from his eyes, wanted to show Sean that he wasn't a disappointment, that she cared deeply about him. To do that, she kissed him with all of the passion coursing through her veins. And when he groaned into her mouth, as if he was consumed with pleasure, Robyn knew she'd made the right decision.

* * *

Manhattan Beach was overrun with families, couples who couldn't keep their paws off each other and loud, irreverent teenagers, but Robyn was enjoying herself so much she didn't mind the noise. She was with Sean at her favorite beach, and they were having a blast. They played in the water for hours, splashing and joking around, then packed up and headed north.

The Venice Boardwalk was a human zoo, filled with performers, eccentric street vendors and tourists. The scent of nachos and cotton candy filled the salty air, and when Sean suggested they eat at one of the nearby restaurants, Robyn agreed. "Good idea," she said. "I'm starving."

"What are you in the mood for?"

You mean, besides you between my legs, making me come over and over again?

An image of Sean plunging his erection inside her made Robyn's body flush with heat. She wanted him again, could almost taste his kiss, feel him on top of her. The memories of their night together would be with her forever, for as long as she lived. Robyn wiped her mind clean, willed herself not to go there, but her thoughts took a sensual detour for the second time in minutes when Sean leaned in and rested a hand on the small of her back. Being close to him, having him by her side warmed her all over. From the moment he'd arrived at her condo last night, he'd been affectionate and sweet, and Robyn loved every minute of it. No one had ever spoiled her silly, and it was a heady feeling, one she felt she could never get enough of.

"Hello?" he joked, waving a hand in front of her face. "Is anyone home?"

Robyn laughed, then answered his question. "I'm not picky. I'll eat anything."

"I know just the place. Thai Spice is a thirty-minute walk from here, but it's definitely worth the trip and arguably one of the best Asian restaurants in LA."

"Then lead the way."

Restaurants, yoga studios and art galleries frequented by the rich and famous lined the busy streets, and animated conversation filled the air. Holding hands, they laughed and kissed as they walked down the road, oblivious to the world around them.

Conversation flowed from one subject to the next, and Robyn loved hearing about Sean's overseas travel. He was a great storyteller, who seemed to get a kick out of making her laugh, but when he opened up about his fears, she felt closer to him than ever before.

"I can't believe it's already four o'clock," she said, glancing at her Gucci bangle watch. It had been a Christmas gift from Kim, and every time Robyn looked at it, she thought about her beautiful bestie. She wished she could tell Kim about her dream date with Sean, but—

"Do you mind if we stop by my restaurant later?" he asked. "I promised Jolene I'd return her car tonight, and I want to keep my word."

"Of course. No problem."

Pride filled his eyes. "I can give you a tour of the SP Grill if you'd like."

"I'd love that." Robyn was having a great time with Sean, and she'd like nothing more than to continue their day. But thoughts of work kept intruding on her fun, especially her upcoming meeting with Enrique Salazar. It loomed in her mind like a dark storm cloud. In the three years she'd been the lead event planner at the Belleza, she'd done it all—corporate events, weddings, bar mitzvahs and baby showers. Lavish, over-the-top parties were her specialty, so a five-hundred-guest birthday bash was right up her alley. Nailing the Salazar presentation was key, and once Robyn returned to the Belleza, she was rolling up her sleeves and getting down to work. "What time are we going to Posh Lounge?"

"Around seven o'clock. Why?"

"Because I have a presentation to finish up," she said. "I'll be burning the midnight oil for the next couple nights, but if I get the contract, it will totally be worth it."

"I'm not taking you back to the resort tonight."

Robyn raised an eyebrow. "Really? Why not?"

"Because you're spending the night with me."

"My, my, my," she quipped. "Aren't we bossy?"

"Not bossy, just determined." Sean stopped walking and turned to face her. "I want to spend time with you. Is that a crime?"

Everything in her wanted to argue, to tell him all the reasons they couldn't be together, but when he brushed his mouth against hers, the protest died on her lips. Weakened by his touch and his passionate kiss, she needed a moment before she could form a coherent sentence. "Sean," she finally said, "we've discussed this before. I can't. It's too risky."

"We don't work together anymore," he pointed out, tightening his hold around her waist.

"But you're estranged from your family, and that complicates matters."

"Not to me. You are, and always will be, the only woman I want."

"Let's just take things one day at a time."

"Why? I know what I want, and baby, it's you."

"Things are moving too fast…" Her throat closed up, and she trailed off. In her peripheral vision, she spotted a slim, attractive blonde in a fuchsia bikini top and itty-bitty jean shorts. It was Charlene, and she wasn't alone. *In bed sick my ass,* Robyn thought, watching the hostess kiss the man she recognized as the French film star. He was a married father of three who brought his young family to the resort every year for Christmas. Wait till Kim and Gabby hear about this.

Are you going to tell them you were with Sean when you spotted Charlene? asked her inner voice. *If not, then keep your big mouth shut.*

Shame colored Robyn's cheeks, and remorse flooded her body. It was time to get down off her high horse and not a moment too soon. She had no right to judge Charlene. Not after sleeping with Sean and smuggling him out of her condo. Sure, she wasn't guilty for having an affair with a married man, but she was guilty of deceiving her best friends, and that wasn't cool. In all the years she'd been friends with Kim and Gabby, she'd never lied to them, and now she felt horrible about sneaking around with Sean behind their backs, especially Kim.

Robyn watched the couple cross the street, and panic swelled inside her chest. If Charlene saw her with Sean there'd be hell to pay, and since Robyn didn't want to lose the best job she'd ever had, she ducked into a souvenir shop and hid behind a rack of designer sunglasses.

"Robyn, what are you doing?"

"Isn't it obvious?" Grabbing a shopping basket, she hurled key chains, magnets and postcards inside. "I'm getting some souvenirs for my mom."

"Why? She lives in Palm Springs now."

Robyn peered over his shoulder, noticed Charlene and

the Frenchman were nowhere in sight and sighed in relief. Putting down the basket, she told Sean she'd changed her mind about buying souvenirs and followed him out of the store.

Minutes later, they arrived at Thai Spice, and were promptly seated at a corner booth beside the window. Sipping Iced Watermelon, Robyn took in her surroundings. The temple-like interior, dragon-design wallpaper and hand-painted silk chandeliers made her feel as if she'd been transported to another world. The spicy aromas wafting out of the open kitchen made her mouth water and her stomach growl in hungry anticipation. "This place is a nice," Robyn said after they'd placed their orders with the waiter. "Have you been here before?"

"Only a million times." Wearing a wry smile, he leaned back comfortably in the booth. "When I was a kid, my mom would bring us to Venice Beach often, and we'd spend the day swimming, playing games and chasing each other around the boardwalk."

"Your dad never came?"

"He came once, and it was a disaster."

"The boardwalk isn't for everybody," Robyn said, feeling the need to defend her former boss. She'd never been close to Kurt Parker, but he'd always treated her with respect, and she admired his tireless work ethic. "It's noisy, crowded and filled with some very odd characters."

"That wasn't it. It was me."

Curious, she leaned forward in her seat.

"I ate too much junk food that day and got sick on the roller coaster," he explained. "My dad said I was an embarrassment to our family, and reamed me out in front of a crowd of people. He used to say 'Without discipline you'll never amount to anything,' and according to him, it was his job to keep me in line."

Robyn felt a flood of emotions—anger, pity, sadness— and struggled to find her voice. "That's terrible," she said, reaching out and touching his hand. She hurt for him, was heartsick over his confession and wanted him to know that she cared. "What did your mom do?"

"What could she do? That was the Kurt Parker way. I was the oldest. I had to be taught a lesson so Kim and Ryan wouldn't make the same stupid mistakes."

"Is that what your father told you? That he had to make an example out of you?"

"He didn't have to. I was punished constantly, no matter how small the infraction. If I woke up late for school, I was punished, if I brought home an A-minus on my report card, I was punished, if I left my basketball in the driveway, I was punished." His eyes narrowed, and his lips were pressed together in suppressed anger. "If it wasn't for my mom, I probably would have run away from home and joined the military."

"Really? Things were that bad between you and your dad?"

Sean nodded. "That's why I took off for Paris after I graduated from high school. The more distance between me and my father the better."

"I knew your dad was strict, but I had no idea you guys had such a strained relationship. You always seemed so close, especially during social functions at the resort."

"That's what Kurt wanted people to think. On the outside looking in, it seems like we're the perfect, all-American family, but we're not."

His words gave her pause, made Robyn think about her own father. They hadn't spoken in months, not since he was a no-show at her surprise birthday party in January, but for some reason, hearing about the Parker family problems made Robyn think her relationship with her dad could be salvaged. Robyn had made mistakes in college and, eight years later, he was still holding a grudge. Should she try reaching out to him again? One last time?

"Kurt and I have never been close, not the way he's close to Kim. In his eyes, she can do no wrong, and that will never change." Anger clouded his face, seeped into his tone. "Kim's a daddy's girl all the way, but it wasn't until she betrayed me that I realized how selfish she is."

"Sean, don't."

Confusion wrinkled his forehead. "Don't what?"

"Don't talk about your sister that way. It's disrespectful."

Robyn felt bad that Sean and Kurt didn't have a good relationship, but she wasn't going to sit back and let him bad-mouth her best friend. Kim had taken Robyn under her wing at Merriweather Academy and made sure no one pushed her around, and she'd always be grateful to Kim and Gabby for having her back. The waiter arrived with their entrées, and Robyn picked up her fork.

"You're right," he said. "I'm sorry for what I said earlier. I was completely out of line."

"Apology accepted."

He smiled, and Robyn did, too.

"How's my favorite chef doing?" he asked, his eyes filled with amusement. "Is she running The Pearl with an iron fist the way I taught her?"

"Gabby's great. She's engaged to a terrific guy and flourishing at the restaurant."

"I'm happy for her. I always knew she had what it took to be an executive chef, and her commitment to excellence will take her far in the field." Sean picked up his glass and took a sip. "Is she getting married at the resort, too?"

"I'm not sure. Gabby's super busy with The Pearl, and when she's not working, she's plotting with Kim to find me a husband, so there's no telling when she'll tie the knot."

Alarm flashed in his eyes, caused lines to wrinkle his handsome face. "Is that right?"

"Yeah, now that they're both happy in love, they're hell-bent on setting me up," Robyn complained. She tasted her cashew nut chicken and decided it was her new favorite dish.

"Tell them you're not interested," he advised.

"I tried, and it backfired in my face."

"What happened?"

"A couple weeks ago, Kim and Gabby asked me to meet them at the Ruby Retreat for lunch, but when I showed up, they weren't there. The next thing I know, a middle-aged man with a South African accent is kissing my hand and pulling out my chair. Apparently, he'd asked Gabby about me, and she arranged the whole thing."

"I'm going to have to call and talk some sense into that girl."

Robyn laughed. "Cool your heels, Sean. I can handle it."

"You better, or I will."

His take-charge demeanor aroused her, and when their eyes met across the table, Robyn knew they shared the same thought. *Check, please!*

Chapter 10

"After you, Ms. Henderson." Wearing a devilish grin, Sean unlocked the front door of the SP Grill and stepped aside to let Robyn enter. Mesmerized by her sexy strut, he stood transfixed, thinking about all the delicious things he wanted to do to her in bed. Her turquoise dress was made for her figure, fit every sinuous curve, and he couldn't help reaching out and caressing her hips. He wanted Robyn to spend the night with him, couldn't imagine anything he'd like more.

He'd left Thai Spice, anxious to return to his place to make love to Robyn, but when she mentioned how much she loved the music at Posh Lounge, he'd driven there instead. They'd had a great time talking and laughing over appetizers and drinks. While they were heating things up on the dance floor, he'd asked her again to spend the night at his place, but she'd declined. Sean was disappointed, especially in light of all the bumping and grinding and kissing they'd done in the private VIP room, but he wasn't giving up. He reflected on last night, on how she'd responded passionately to him in the bedroom, and the more he thought about their erotic experience, the more he wanted her. Desired her. Craved her. Itched to make love to her again, and again, and again.

"Sean, is that you?"

Hearing Jolene's voice, he abandoned his thoughts and clasped Robyn's hand. He led her through the dimly lit dining room and into the bright and spacious kitchen. It was spotless, just the way he liked, and a rich, savory aroma filled the air.

"Hey, Sean. It's good to see you." Jolene peeled off her rubber gloves, dropped them on the counter, and straightened her too-tight, sleeveless dress. "How was your day off?"

"Great," he said, returning her smile. "Jolene, this is my girlfriend, Robyn."

"Girlfriend?" She scrunched up her nose, as if she'd just gotten a whiff of rotten milk and puckered her lips. Then, as if she'd just caught herself, she smiled. "Well, isn't that wonderful? Welcome to the SP Grill, Robyn."

"Thanks. It's nice to meet you."

"I need you to help me convince Robyn to join our team," Sean said, winking good-naturedly at his assistant. "She's a top-notch event planner, and we could use someone with her skill and expertise."

Both women stared at him with wide eyes, and a long, awkward silence ensued.

"Are you hungry?" With a flick of her hand, Jolene gestured to the industrial stove. "I made salmon ravioli and left it warming in the oven. Go ahead, help your-selves."

"We're good. Take it home to your kids. I'm sure they'll love it."

Her face softened, brightened with happiness. "Thanks, Sean. That's very sweet of you."

"You should get going. You did a double shift today, and I bet you're exhausted."

Jolene shook her head. "I don't mind staying to give you a rundown of the day."

"No worries. We can talk in the morning." Sean handed Jolene her car keys, scooped his up off the counter and dropped them in his shirt pocket. "I'll be here bright and early, unless I can convince Robyn to spend the night. Then I won't be in at all."

Sean laughed, but no one else did. Jolene looked pissed, as if someone had cut her off on the freeway, and Robyn dropped his hand. Apparently he'd done something wrong, but what?

"Good night." Jolene grabbed her purse off the counter and left the kitchen.

Sean opened his mouth to ask Robyn what was wrong, but she spoke first.

"Why did you tell your assistant that we're a couple?" she demanded, an angry scowl bruising her lips. "What if Jolene says something next time your mom drops by? Do you know what would happen if Kim found out about us? Do you even care?"

"I don't understand why you're upset."

"Of course you don't! All you care about is sticking it to Kim, but I won't let you use me in this sick, twisted game you're playing. I'm out of here."

"Oh, no you're not."

"Just watch me."

Robyn spun around on her heels, but Sean caught her around the waist and pulled her back into his arms before she could flee the kitchen. "I hate when you talk like that."

"And I hate when you embarrass me," she shot back.

Arguing with Robyn made Sean hot under the collar. It also awakened other senses. Seeing the heat flare in her eyes made him recall how she'd responded to him last night. The urge to kiss her right then was so over-whelming it was all he could think about. Lust consumed him, coursed furiously through his veins. He lowered his mouth to do just that, but she turned her face away.

"I told you I'm not ready to go public with our rela-tionship. I love and need my job, and if we go public I could lose everything I've worked hard for."

"We're too old to be sneaking around," he said firmly. "That's kids' stuff, Robyn."

"Why do you have to be so stubborn?"

"And why do you have to be so sexy?"

A smile tickled the corners of her lips, and Sean knew if he made her laugh he'd be out of the doghouse in no time. He searched her eyes for answers and felt a tight-ening sensation in his chest, a rush of emotion. It wasn't the right time to bare his soul, but one day soon, he'd tell Robyn the truth, everything that was in his heart. He only hoped when he said those three little words that she'd return the sentiment.

"I told Jolene you're my girlfriend because that's who you are. My girl. And I don't give a damn who knows."

"Well, I do. We have to keep a low profile until the police figure out who's trying to destroy the Belleza and put the culprit behind bars, where he belongs."

"Baby, it's not that serious. We can openly date. It's not like you're in the witness protection program!"

Robyn laughed, and his chest inflated with pride. Sean loved making her smile, felt ten feet tall every time she laughed and got a kick out of spoiling her. After their scrumptious, three-hour lunch at Thai Spice, he'd treated her to a shopping spree at a ritzy Venice boutique known for its cutting-edge designs. With encouragement, she'd modeled several outfits for him, everything from lingerie to designer gowns, and since everything looked amazing on her, he'd purchased them all. Robyn protested, argued that she could buy her own clothes, but he'd given the cashier his platinum credit card anyway and carried the garment bags to the car.

"We'll do things your way for now, but—" Sean heard his cell phone ring, knew from the ringtone that it was his brother calling and broke off speaking. He hadn't talked to him in weeks and wanted to touch base with him. "It's Ryan. Do you mind if I take this call?"

"Not at all. Take as long as you need."

Sean swiped his index finger across the screen and put his cell to his ear. "Hey, bro, what's up? It's been a long time," he said good-naturedly. "How's the Big Apple treating you?"

"Not bad. How are things going at the restaurant?"

"Great. I was just about to give Robyn a—"

Robyn waved her hands furiously back and forth. "Don't tell Ryan I'm here," she whispered. "Word could get back to Kim."

"Sean? Hello? Are you there?"

"Yeah, sorry, bro." Sean gave his head a shake and tore his gaze away from Robyn's luscious lips. She was the ultimate distraction, the sweetest piece of eye candy he'd ever seen, and he had to force himself to stop staring at her. "How was your gig in Tribeca last weekend?"

"Terrible. The club owner gypped me out of five hundred bucks," he complained, a bitter edge in his voice. "Needless to say, I won't be performing there again."

"Do you need another loan?"

"No, I'm straight, but thanks for asking."

"You're still coming to my grand opening, right?"

"Wouldn't miss it for the world," Ryan said. "My manager got me a gig in Long Beach this month, and I was hoping you'd come out. I know you'll be crazy-busy getting ready for your grand opening, but it would be cool to see a friendly face in the audience."

"I'll be there." Sean made a mental note to deposit some money into Ryan's bank account, as well. Years ago, Ryan had been in charge of entertainment at the resort, but his dreams had always extended beyond the Belleza's borders, and Sean was proud of him for finally stepping out on his own. Naturally, their parents were disappointed in Ryan's decision to pursue a music career—especially their father—but Sean supported his brother wholeheartedly.

"I'll text you the details later this week," Ryan said.

"Is it okay if I bring my girl to your show?"

"Your girl? You're kidding, right?"

"I'm dating someone." Sean stared at Robyn, saw her eyes widen, the flicker of surprise that flashed across her pretty face. He wanted to take her in his arms and devour her but knew if he kissed her he wouldn't be able to stop. "I think she could be the one, bro."

"That's hard to believe. You're so scared of commitment you haven't had a girlfriend since first grade," he joked, releasing a deep belly laugh. "Bring her along. I *have* to meet her."

They spoke for a few more minutes, about their parents, the resort and preseason football, but as soon as Sean ended the call, he reached for Robyn. Her radiant smile was a turn-on, her curvy, delectable figure, too. He more than liked what he saw, and he wanted her so bad he couldn't stop from caressing her body. The chemistry between them was undeniable, an unstoppable force he couldn't resist any longer. Consumed with desire, he ravished her mouth. Tickling her tongue with the tip of his own, he cupped her breasts with his hands and rubbed his erection against her sex.

"Hold it right there." Breaking off the kiss, Robyn pressed her hands flat against his chest and gave him a stern look. "You promised me a tour *and* a slice of coconut cake, and I'm going to hold you to your word."

Sean chuckled and gave her a peck on the cheek. He liked being around Robyn, and her saucy personality and cheeky wit excited him. "Let the tour begin…"

Walking through the restaurant with Robyn at his side made his heart race. He wanted to impress her, desired her approval and hoped she liked what she saw. Inspired by his travels abroad, he'd created a warm, sprawling space filled with chandeliers, lush tapestries and contemporary furniture, all in a burgundy color scheme. "What do you think?"

Her eyes were filled with awe. "This place is incredible."

"You think so?"

"Are you kidding me? It reeks of wealth, and I have a feeling it's going to be a celebrity hot spot in no time," she predicted, running a hand along the mahogany bar. "You're a talented chef, and once word gets out that you own the SP Grill, it'll be packed from wall to wall."

Satisfaction and relief flowed through his body. "Thanks, Robyn. I hope you're right."

"Boy, please. I'm *always* right!"

They laughed, and continued through the lounge, discussing the sultry ambience and decor.

"Are you planning something big for the grand opening?" Robyn asked.

"I'm working on it. I have a few ideas in mind but nothing concrete yet."

"Is Ryan performing?"

Sean frowned, scratched his head. "Performing what?"

"With his band. I naturally assumed he'd perform, him being your brother and all." She added, "And, a very talented musician, as well."

"To be honest, I never thought of it."

"You should. Ryan has an amazing voice, and he puts on one hell of a show."

"I'll think about it." Taking her hand, he led her through the darkened lounge, down the corridor, and past the private dining room. Sean opened his office door, stepped inside and turned on the light. "This is my home away from home."

Robyn whistled. "This isn't an office. It's a bachelor pad."

Knowing he'd be spending long days at the SP Grill, he'd commissioned his Malaysian-born architect to create the office of his dreams. And she'd delivered big-time. It had a sitting area, complete with couches, padded chairs and end tables; a full bathroom and walk-in closet; and a sixty-inch plasma TV mounted to the wall. His eyes trailed Robyn as she moved around the office, admiring the aquarium, the sculptures and his numerous culinary awards.

"Wow, what a great shot," Robyn gushed, pointing at the framed photograph sitting on the bookshelf. "I love this picture of you and your family."

Me, too, Sean thought but didn't say. The picture had been taken at the Belleza last year during the Christmas holidays, and every time he looked at it, he felt a sharp pang in his chest—especially when his gaze fell across his sister. He'd read about Kim and Jaxon Dunham in the society pages of the local newspaper, but he still couldn't believe they were an item. Kim hadn't had a serious boyfriend in years and was too busy working at the resort to date, so her surprise engagement to the Dunham heir blew his mind.

"I love having you here." Sean moved closer, erased the distance between them. Coming up behind her, he kissed the back of her neck and wrapped his arms around her waist. "I could get used to this. You, being here with me, 24/7."

Robyn smiled and said, "Thanks for everything. I had a great day with you."

"The night's still young. There's plenty more fun to be had."

"Sean, I have to get back to the resort—"

He crushed his lips against hers and wrapped her up in his arms. They kissed passionately, made sweet love to each other's mouths. Sean slipped a hand underneath her sundress, ran his hands along her thighs, hips and across her navel. "You feel so damn good."

Robyn purred, groaned in agony as he stroked and massaged her flesh. He was sweating profusely, burning up. He wanted her so bad he couldn't think of anything but making love to her. He had to have her, right then and there, before he exploded inside his boxers.

Lust covered her face, twinkled in her pretty hazel eyes. She didn't speak, didn't utter a word, but her body language spoke volumes. She wanted him, too. No doubt about it. He sensed it, felt it, knew it without a doubt. She knew how to move, how to rock her hips and ass, and her sensuous, erotic moves made his erection throb inside his pants.

Sean licked her bottom lip with his tongue, slowly sucked on it. "Strip for me."

"No way! I could never do something like that."

"Why not? You're the sexiest woman I know."

"And you're too slick for your own good."

"Come on, baby. Don't make me beg."

Robyn giggled and rolled her eyes to the ceiling. "You're crazy."

"You're right," he conceded, his voice a husky growl. "I'm crazy about you."

She gave him a kiss sizzling with heat as she stroked his shoulders and chest. "You're not calling the shots tonight. *I* am."

Her hungry stare and sultry tone surprised him. The first time they'd made love she'd been shy, nervous even, about him seeing her naked body, but tonight she seemed to be imbued with confidence, and her boldness made him want her even more.

Robyn unzipped his pants, tossed his belt aside and pushed him down onto his leather executive chair. She dropped to her knees, pulled down his boxer briefs, and before Sean knew what was happening, she had his erection inside her mouth. Her tongue slid down his length, tickled the tip of his shaft. *Hot damn. How did she learn to do that?*

Sean kept his gaze on her, felt himself harden like steel as he watched Robyn do her thing. Their eyes met, bore into each other. Her come-hither look was lethal, her tongue action unlike anything he'd ever experienced. Without a doubt, the sexiest thing he'd ever seen. She knew what he wanted sexually, and she gave him exactly what he needed, what his horny body was craving. His toes curled inside his shoes, and Sean knew that his orgasm was right around the corner.

"Do you have a condom?"

He'd come prepared, had three flavored condoms tucked inside his wallet and planned to use them all tonight. He took one out, chucked his wallet on the desk and rolled it down his erection.

Sean watched with wide eyes, as Robyn took off her sundress and dropped it on the floor. She stood in front of him, in a purple satin bra and thong, and the sight of her creamy brown skin against the bright, shiny material made his mouth water with hunger. "Come here." Sean pulled her to him and gripped her hips. He kissed her navel, flicked his tongue greedily against it. "Turn around, baby. I want to see every inch of you."

Pride brightened her eyes, warmed her face, and Sean knew he'd said the right thing. As she spun around for him, Robyn unhooked her bra, twirled it in the air and tossed it at him. He loved her sensuous strip tease, ate it up. Her thong was the next to go, and as he watched the flimsy material slide down her thighs, he reached out and rubbed her ass. It was a thing of beauty. Plump, juicy, made for squeezing, and he loved how it fit perfectly in his hands.

His erection grew, doubled in length. Sean couldn't

take it anymore. He was dying for release. He pulled Robyn down on his lap, positioned his erection against her sex and sucked her nipple into his mouth. He licked it, kissed it, lapped his tongue against it as if it was a juicy piece of fruit. "Ride me hard and fast, and don't stop until I tell you to."

"Is that a challenge?" Robyn lowered herself onto his erection, gripped the back of his chair and got to work. Her ardor and intensity were shocking. The last thing he'd ever expected. Raising her legs, she rocked back and forth, swiveled her hips as if she was playing with a hula hoop. Their bodies slapped hard against each other, and the wild, primal sound brought out the beast in him. He nipped her earlobe, trailed kisses down the front of her neck.

Excitement built, filled every inch of his office, consumed the air. His hands explored. Robyn moaned her pleasure, told him how much she desired him. Sean found himself opening up to her, too. Everything with Robyn felt right, as natural as breathing, and the sex was so damn good he couldn't imagine ever making love to anyone else.

She laced her fingers with his as they moved together as one, lavished each other with kisses and caresses. "I love the way you make me feel," she whispered hoarsely. "Don't stop. *Please* don't stop."

But he did. Sean stood up, carried Robyn over to his desk, and laid her flat on her back. He positioned his shaft against her sex, slid it slowly back and forth against the treasure between her thighs. Sexing Robyn on top of his desk was a dream come true, an erotic fantasy he'd replay in his mind for many years to come. He entered her in one swift, fluid motion, then thrust his erection so deep inside her she screamed his name. Robyn spread her legs wide, as if inviting him in. She arched her pelvis upward to receive each thrust. He dove into her, over and over again, so powerfully the pictures on his desk crashed to the floor.

"Turn around."

Robyn did a slow turn. Bracing her hands against the desk, she swiveled and swirled her butt against his crotch. The view from behind was jaw-dropping. His hands slid down her sides, caressed the small of her back, her hips, then cupped her beautiful big breasts. It was his new favorite position, the one he'd see every time he closed his eyes.

Sean slapped her ass, grinned when she moaned out loud. He did it again. Same results, only this time her voice carried around the room, bouncing off the walls, windows and ceiling. The sound was the most erotic thing he'd ever heard, music to his ears.

Their lovemaking was intense, explosive, like something in an X-rated movie, hands-down the best sex of his life. A climax overtook her body, caused Robyn to buck against him. That's when all hell broke loose, and Sean lost control.

Pleasure erupted inside him, set off explosive fireworks. Sex was the ultimate high, the greatest rush, and he came powerfully, with such intensity he feared he'd black out. Exhausted but content, he dropped onto his leather chair, and pulled Robyn down onto his lap.

"You're amazing," he breathed.

"You're not too bad yourself."

"You're going to be the death of me," he groaned. "We just finished, but I want you again."

Robyn cocked her head to the right, as if deep in thought, and tapped an index finger to her temple. "What's that saying about too much of a good thing?"

"Hell if I know, because I could never, ever get enough of you."

Sean kissed her forehead, the tip of her nose, caressed her shoulders and back. A smile shaped her lips, and she cocooned herself in the crux of his arms. He was in no rush to leave, could stay there with Robyn forever, but he saw the time on the clock and knew it was time to take her back to the resort. "I better take you home," he said, brushing the hair away from her face. "I don't want the Iron Lady to fire you for missing curfew."

"I'm not going home."

"You're not?"

"Nope. I'm spending the night with you, remember?"

"That's right. You are."

His thoughts raced, shifted into overdrive. Sean wanted to make Robyn feel special tonight, wanted to take care of her and decided he'd run her a hot bath when they returned to his house. Robyn was just his type, perfect for him in every way, and he wasn't going to mess things up with her. Not this time. Not when they were closer than ever. The sex was outstanding, sure, but his feelings for her had little to do with sex, and everything to do with who she was as a person— considerate, loyal, someone he could depend on. He could always count on her, trusted her explicitly and knew she'd never do anything to hurt him. Sean recognized what was at stake, and he knew what he was up against. He had to prove to Robyn that he was for real, that he wouldn't hurt her. He only hoped Kim and his parents wouldn't thwart his plans, because he had a goal in sight: to make Robyn Mrs. Sean Parker, and no one was going to stand in his way.

Chapter 11

"Robyn, are you okay? You've been acting strange the past two weeks, and I want to know why."

Raising her eyes up from her mat, Robyn chanced a look at Kim. Big mistake. Her best friend was staring at her intently, watching her every move. Her heart pounded with fear, thundered violently in her ears. *Is she on to me? Does she know I've been seeing Sean on the sly? Is the truth written all over my face?* Their 6:00 a.m. Pilates class had just wrapped up, and Robyn had hoped to escape the session without being interrogated by Kim, but no such luck.

"Sorry for being preoccupied this morning, but my meeting with Enrique Salazar is this afternoon. If I don't nail this presentation, he might take his business to The Pinnacle. I can't stop thinking about it."

Liar! yelled her inner voice. *Sean is the one you can't stop thinking about.*

It was true, he was, but Robyn couldn't tell Kim she'd fallen for her estranged brother. Not today. Likely, not ever.

"Did you get the message I sent you about the changes to the menu for the Rabinowitz anniversary party?" Gabby asked, breaking in to their conversation. "It's not extensive, but I'd still like you to look at it."

"No, sorry. I was busy last night and didn't get a chance to read it."

Kim frowned. "Really? But that's so unlike you. You're *always* checking your work email."

Not anymore, Robyn thought, patting back a yawn. Even though she'd canceled with Sean last night, they'd talked on the phone for hours and she'd slept in this morning. It was a wonder she'd even made it to class.

"Give me a shout after you've read it so I can order the necessary supplies."

"Will do," she said, uncrossing her legs and putting on her Skechers slip-on shoes. Robyn was exhausted, but she was glad she'd attended the class with her friends. All week, she'd been sneaking off to see Sean after work, and when they weren't hanging out at his swank bachelor pad, they were burning up the airwaves. She hardly saw Kim and Gabby anymore, but tomorrow she was going to treat her best friends to manicures and pedicures in the resort spa.

Robyn glanced at her watch, calculated the hours until she'd see Sean. They were going to the LA Food and Wine Festival in LA, then to the Usher concert at the Staples Center. And that wasn't all. He'd scored them backstage passes, too.

She was so anxious to see Sean, she could hardly wait for six o'clock to roll around. Her outfit was already hanging on her closet door, and she couldn't wait to see the look on Sean's face when he saw her in the metallic, one-shoulder dress. He'd bought it for her while shopping at the Venice Boardwalk, and the moment she'd stepped out of the fitting room his face had lit up. He'd mentioned her wearing the outfit to his grand opening, but since Robyn wasn't attending that event, she'd wear it tonight for their date.

Robyn cleared her mind, returned to the present. She had to stop daydreaming about Sean, had to focus on the here and now. She'd do her presentation, meet briefly with her staff to discuss the Dunham Foundation gala, then head straight to LA.

Robyn stood, rolled up her mat and tucked it under her forearm. "I wish I could stick around for the next class, but I have a million things to do between now and lunch."

"Same here," Gabby said, rising to her feet, her lush, loose curls bouncing around her face. Her pink workout attire fit her body perfectly and complimented her creamy brown skin tone. "Kim, are you staying?"

"And let Xander kill me with his impossible cardio circuit? Hell, no!"

Laughing, the women collected their things and headed for the exit.

"You were supposed to meet me at The Pearl for drinks last night. What happened?"

Robyn glanced at the door just in time to see Charlene sashay into the room in a belly-baring shirt, cotton shorts and wedge sandals. Like the other women in the class, she had a crush on the Greek instructor and flirted with him every chance she got. Just last week Charlene was at Venice Beach, draped all over that French film star, and now she was chasing down Xander. The woman sure got around, Robyn thought.

She watched as Charlene made her move. In her haste to reach the fitness instructor, the hostess tripped and fell flat on her face. Without missing a beat, she popped back up on her feet, flicked her hair over her shoulders and pranced across the room. Charlene had more game than a Williams sister and the curvy figure to match.

"That girl is something else," Robyn said, marveling at the blonde's latest blunder. "She'll do *anything* for male attention."

"Did I tell you guys about the time Charlene propositioned Sean in The Pearl after closing?" Gabby asked them. "If he hadn't texted me to come rescue him, she probably would have devoured him."

Robyn's eyes narrowed, and her hands balled into fists. The next time Charlene made a move on Sean, she'd be eating a knuckle sandwich. Charlene had helped her out considerably over the last few days, and Robyn was grateful, but that didn't mean she was going to stand by and let Charlene put the moves on her man.

My man, she thought, sighing dreamily. *I just love the sound of that. And his kisses, too!*

Kim's voice broke into her thoughts. "I bet my brother encouraged her advances. I wouldn't put anything past him."

Robyn linked arms with her friend as they exited the fitness center. "Kim, you should try calling Sean again. I bet he's finally come around and desperate to patch things up."

"Girl, please, I'd rather go six rounds with Laila Ali!"

Kim and Gabby laughed, but Robyn didn't see anything funny about Sean being estranged from his family.

He acted as if he didn't miss his parents or sister, but she suspected he was miserable without them. "You should reach out to him one last time."

"No way. He's selfish and petty, and I don't care if I ever see him again."

Gabby gasped. "Kim, don't say things like that."

"Why not? It's true. I idolized Sean my entire life, but he abandoned me instead of supporting me, and if that wasn't bad enough he turned Ryan against me, too."

"Ryan has a mind of his own, and I seriously doubt Sean or anyone else has any control over him," Robyn argued, climbing into the golf cart they'd used to travel from the staff condos to the fitness center. "Next time he's in town have a heart-to-heart talk with him."

"You're right. I should. Ryan isn't so bad. It's Sean I have issues with." Kim slipped on her diamond-encrusted, Dior sunglasses and sat behind the wheel. "Would you guys believe my mom drove all the way to the SP Grill and Sean refused to talk to her?"

"Y-you're mom told you that?" Robyn stammered, her eyes wide with shock.

"She didn't have to. I read between the lines."

Robyn wanted to tell Kim that she was wrong, that Sean had been caring and sweet when he spoke to Ilene on the phone, but wisely bit her tongue. Defending him would raise suspicion, and furthermore, Robyn didn't want Kim to think she was taking sides.

"Apparently your brother has a hot, new girlfriend."

Robyn gaped at Gabby, and Kim asked, "Gabby, who told you that?"

"No one. I saw it on his Facebook page. I go on it periodically to check up on him, and yesterday, I noticed he'd changed his status from 'Single' to 'In a Relationship,' and that's not all." Gabby swiped her finger across her cell phone, typed for several seconds, then turned to face her friends. "This is what Sean posted on his page this morning. 'The woman of my dreams has been sitting under my nose for more than a decade, and tonight, I'm going to prove to her that she is, and always will be, the only woman for me.'"

He did what? Robyn was glad she was sitting down, because if she'd been standing, she would have fallen to the ground. It took a moment for her to compose herself. Sean had agreed to keep their relationship a secret, so Robyn didn't understand his public declaration. She didn't know whether to be honored or annoyed. Why would he post that message on Facebook? Didn't he know Kim would see it?

"I hope Sean didn't get back together with Trina, because I can't stand her," Kim said.

"Me, too, but who else could it be?" Gabby asked, scratching her head. "They've known each other since high school, and she's been head over heels in love with him for years."

Scared of being dragged into the conversation, Robyn took her cell out of her gym bag and logged on to her email. She pretended to be reading, but she was listening intently to what her friends were saying. Did Sean mean what he'd posted online? Robyn wondered, more confused than ever. Was he serious about her, or was he trying to get back at Kim?

The woman in question waved her hands. "I don't want to talk about Sean anymore. It's bringing me down. Let's discuss my fabulous, Jack and Jill wedding shower," Kim said enthusiastically, a radiant smile on her face. She turned on the golf cart and took off like a rocket down the winding trail. It was lush, green and lined with soaring palm trees. "Robyn, are you bringing a date?"

"Yes, of course. It just so happens that Shemar Moore is available." Robyn waved her cell phone in the air. "He just sent me a text to confirm."

Gabby laughed and flashed a thumbs-up. "Good one, Robyn."

"You need to get some and fast," Kim said matter-of-factly, jabbing her friend in the ribs with her elbow. "It's been, what? Eight, nine years? That's why you're so cynical about men, but don't worry, it's nothing a night of toe-curling sex can't fix."

I couldn't have said it better myself, Robyn thought, hiding a smirk. *I haven't been able to stop smiling since I made love to Sean. And he's certainly cured my insomnia. Now, I sleep like a baby.*

Her friends chatted excitedly about wedding favors and flower arrangements, but Robyn tuned them out. As they drove through the grounds she admired the tall, majestic mountains surrounding the resort. There was a plethora of hiking trails around the Belleza, and whenever Robyn needed to clear her head, she escaped to the peace and tranquility of the great outdoors.

Soaking in the sunshine, Robyn breathed in the fresh air. It couldn't be a more beautiful day. Hummingbirds soared in the sky, the breeze carried the sweet-smelling scent of tropical fruits, and vibrant flowers brightened the grounds.

Hearing water splashing and high-pitched giggles, Robyn glanced at the pool area. Comfy lounge chairs, cabanas and flotation devices were everywhere. Her gaze landed on the clear blue water, and her thoughts turned to Sean.

A smile bloomed in her heart, and her skin tingled. Her body flushed with heat when she remembered their last sexual encounter. After a delicious home-cooked meal, Sean had made her fantasies come true. While swimming in his backyard pool, he'd captured her around the waist, backed her up against the wall and kissed her hard on the mouth. Untying her bikini, he'd praised her curves and ravished her body with his lips, tongue and hands. He'd slid his erection between her legs, thrust so powerfully she'd begged him not to stop. Sean knew what she wanted, what she needed, and had given it to her over and over again, until an orgasm had stolen her breath.

"I'm a hundred percent committed to you," he'd said, staring deep into her eyes. "I don't want anyone else, Robyn. Only you. And that will never change. Now that I have you, I have everything a man could want."

Days later, she still remembered how sincere he'd sounded, how vulnerable. Their relationship was still new and tender, a couple weeks old, and Robyn was scared of moving too fast. She adored Sean, had since they were teenagers, but she didn't want to upset Kim by confessing the truth. Robyn didn't want to ever have to choose between her best friend and her lover, and she was determined to keep their relationship a secret.

"Home sweet home," Kim said, parking the golf cart at the entrance of the staff condos.

"Jaxon and Geoffrey are taking us to an advance screening of the new Denzel Washington movie tonight. Want to come?"

"So you can set me up with another South African businessman?" Robyn asked. "Hell, no."

Gabby flashed an innocent, good-girl smile. "I was

just trying to get you some, Robyn, but Shemar Moore wasn't available that day!"

Laughing, Robyn waved, hopped off the cart and strode inside her condo. An hour later, she was showered, clad in a multicolored Betsey Johnson dress with capped sleeves and nude leather pumps and back on the golf cart, headed to the main building to check on the preparations for her one o'clock meeting with Enrique Salazar.

The Pearl, with its simple, all-white decor, romantic ambience and chandelier lights, was a visual treat, and as Robyn entered the restaurant she couldn't help noticing all of the kissing couples. Would she and Sean ever be able to hang out there? she wondered. Or would they always have to stay indoors to avoid running into someone they knew? They'd had a close call on the Venice Boardwalk, and now split their time between his home and the SP Grill, but Robyn loved living at the resort and wished they could enjoy its amazing amenities together.

Jonah stood at the bar, decked out in his trademark plaid vest, bowtie and tuxedo shirt. He was laughing heartily with a silver-haired gentleman, but he waved as she walked by.

Entering the private dining room, Robyn was thrilled to see her staff was busy at work, and most important, that they'd followed her instructions to a tee. To wow Enrique Salazar, she'd researched his favorite things, which turned out to be Cristal champagne, Cuban cigars, fine dining and Las Vegas showgirls, and she'd incorporated them into the presentation. She'd bought Charlene and three equally pretty waitresses glitzy showgirl costumes, and Robyn suspected when Enrique saw the stunning quartet he'd sign on the dotted line.

Wanting to check on the food, Robyn spun on her heels, strode down the corridor and poked her head inside the kitchen. It was a frenzy of activity, filled with servers, rushing from one end of the room to the next, and tantalizing aromas. Gabby was standing at the counter, mincing bell peppers and giving orders to the assistant chef.

"How is the mango gazpacho coming along?" Robyn asked, raising her voice to be heard above the whir of the blender. "Will everything be ready by one?"

Gabby vigorously nodded her head. "Absolutely, and I hope Enrique and his entourage are hungry, because I made a double portion of everything, even the empanadas."

"Thanks, girl. You're the best."

Robyn heard her cell phone chime and retrieved it from her dainty side pocket. The message was from Sean, and reading it made her feel irresistible, like the sexiest woman alive. Her smile was so wide her jaw ached, but she couldn't stop grinning from ear-to-ear.

I can't wait to see you. I'm counting down the minutes. Make sure you eat a big lunch, because you're going to need your strength. I'm going to love you all night long.

I hope you do, Robyn thought, licking her lips.

Her cell phone rang, and her heart sped up with excitement. But it wasn't Sean. It was Kim, and Robyn knew why her best friend was calling. Kim wanted to ensure everything was ready in the private dining room for Enrique's impending arrival, and Robyn wouldn't be surprised if Kim had some last-minute suggestions as well. "Hey, girl, what's up?"

"I need you to come to my office right away."

Robyn frowned, stared down at her phone. Kim sounded worried, on edge, unlike her calm, confident self. "Why? What's wrong?" she asked, feeling a flutter of panic in the pit of her stomach. "Is everything okay?"

"No, it's not. Hurry. I'm waiting."

Click.

Fear knotted inside Robyn's chest. Had Kim found out she was secretly dating Sean? Was she going to ask her to leave the resort? Or worse, fire her? Shaking from head to toe, Robyn summoned her courage and marched briskly toward the main building, praying her days as the lead event planner at the Belleza Resort weren't over.

Kim's office was done in bright tones, filled with designer furniture, and had more African-American artwork than the Getty Museum. It wasn't as big as Sean's office at the SP Grill, but it was just as lavish. Glass sculptures, antique bookshelves and the vibrant decor made the space look grand and sophisticated.

Robyn's legs were wobbling, but she walked confidently across the room as if she was on top of her game, in complete control.

"What's up?" Hearing her stomach growl, she grabbed a handful of Skittles from the candy dish on Kim's fuchsia desk and plopped down on one of the padded, leather chairs. "You sounded upset on the phone. Is everything okay?"

"No. I need a *huge* favor."

Robyn sighed in relief. Her secret was safe and so was her job at the Belleza, and since she wanted to keep it that way, she nodded and said, "Sure, of course, what is it?"

"I just got off the phone with Enrique. He's not coming."

"What?" The word exploded out of Robyn's mouth. "What do you mean, he's not coming? I've been working my ass off on the presentation for weeks."

"I know, and I appreciate all your hard work, but I need you to fly to Guadalajara today."

Mexico? But she had a date with Sean.

"I need you to meet with Enrique at his villa," Kim continued, clasping her hands together on her desk. "He's feeling under the weather and requested you make the trip instead."

"Why can't he come here one day next week?"

"I suggested that, but he's travelling to Kuwait on business tomorrow and isn't sure when he'll be back in the States. Furthermore, his thirtieth birthday is six weeks away, and he wants to get the ball rolling now."

"I understand that, Kim, and I agree time is of the essence, but—"

"But what?" she demanded, raising a thin, perfectly arched eyebrow. "To be honest, I'm surprised by your reaction. I thought you'd be excited. You're going to Guadalajara, and it isn't costing you a dime. What could be better than that?"

Having a romantic date with Sean, that's what!

Robyn gripped her armrest, dug her fingernails into the plush leather. Her face must have showed her true feelings—how pissed she was—because Kim wore a sympathetic smile and spoke in a soft, soothing tone, like a mother consoling a child. "Sorry, I know the last-minute change of plans is frustrating, but Enrique's dad and my father are old friends, and if I ignore his request, it'll be seen as an insult, and it might cause tension between our families."

Robyn held her tongue, took a moment to gather her

thoughts. She thought of lying, of telling Kim that her mom was sick at home with pneumonia and that she had to go to Palm Springs to take care of her, but she couldn't bring herself to say the words. Robyn felt trapped, caught between a rock and a hard place, and didn't know what to do.

"Enrique's birthday parties are legendary, attended by the who's who of the business world and tons of A-list stars, and this year I want it here at the resort. Imagine the free publicity we'll get," Kim gushed enthusiastically. "Enrique wants to rent out the entire resort for his guests, and I don't have to tell you what that could mean for the Belleza."

Kim didn't have to remind her. She wanted the contract just as badly as her friend. But she also wanted to be with Sean tonight.

"I hope you don't mind, but I had Antoine make all of your travel arrangements." Kim grabbed a manila envelope off her desk, handed it to Robyn and checked the time on her diamond watch. "You're booked on the eleven-thirty flight to Guadalajara, so you have to hustle. Enrique will send a car to pick you up from the airport and bring you to his private villa."

"I hope I'm flying first class," Robyn said, peeking into the envelope and scanning her two-page travel itinerary. "It's the *least* you can do."

"If you marry that South African businessman, your days of flying commercial would be over, you know. He has his own plane. Not to mention several multimillion dollar properties in California."

"I don't care if he owns the state. I'm still not interested."

"It's time you got back out there, Robyn. I found the

man of my dreams, right here at the resort, and I want the same for you."

The only man I want is Sean. And I can't have him.

"I don't have time to date," Robyn said with a shrug. "I'm too busy with work."

Sure, that was a lie. But what was she going to say? *"I'm dating your brother, and I'm happier than I've ever been?"* She couldn't, not unless she wanted to ruin their friendship. And that was one thing Robyn couldn't stand. Kim and Gabby were the sisters she'd never had, and she couldn't imagine her life without them in it.

Kim shifted uncomfortably in her chair. "There's one last thing…" She fiddled absently with her engagement ring, then finally met Robyn's gaze. "Don't tell Enrique that Sean left the resort. Enrique *loves* my brother's cooking, and if he finds out Sean isn't the executive chef of The Pearl anymore, he might take his business elsewhere, and we can't afford to lose this contract to one of our competitors."

"Are you asking me to lie?"

"No," she said with an impish smile. "I'm asking you to fudge the truth."

Robyn thought about it for a minute, then decided Kim's request made sense. Her loyalty was to the Belleza, and if she wanted to keep her job, she had to support Kim. "Okay, I'll do it," she said, rising to her feet. "I'd better get going."

Kim waved. "Thanks, girl, I owe you one. Have a safe flight."

Twenty minutes later in the privacy of her condo, Robyn called Sean's cell phone. The moment she heard his deep, oh-so-sexy voice, her heart smiled. His dreamy tone aroused her, and several moments passed before Robyn regained her composure.

"I was just about to call you," he said smoothly. "Are you having a good day?"

She had been, until she'd found out she had to fly to Guadalajara.

On the drive back from the main building to her condo, Robyn had rehearsed what she was going to say to Sean, but now that he was on the phone, she couldn't get her thoughts in order. If she told Sean about her meeting with Enrique, it could jeopardize the deal, and she didn't want to let Kim down. "I'm not feeling well," she blurted out, the words falling out of her mouth in a nervous gush. "I think I might be coming down with something."

It was true. She *didn't* feel well. Her heart was racing, and her stomach was in knots. Robyn knew Sean would be pissed if she told him about her trip to Guadalajara, so she told a white lie instead. "I'm going to bed to try to sleep this thing off."

"I'm disappointed, but I understand."

Releasing the breath she'd been holding, Robyn sighed in relief for the second time in minutes. She'd make it up to Sean when she returned from her trip and knew just what to do to get back in his good books. *I'll make him dinner and serve it buck naked.*

"I'm going to make you my famous garlic and kale soup and bring it over tonight. It's packed with veggies and spices and guaranteed to make you feel better."

Robyn spoke without thinking and regretted the words the moment they left her mouth. "No. Don't. You can't come here. It's a bad idea."

"But I want to see you."

"No, not tonight," she said in a calmer voice. "Maybe on the weekend, once I feel better."

The silence lasted so long Robyn knew Sean was mad at her. Her conscience tormented her, but that was nothing new. These days, guilt was her constant companion. She lied to Kim so her best friend wouldn't find out she was dating Sean and kept secrets from Sean so he wouldn't know she was lying to clients about him leaving the resort. *You've created a fine mess this time,* pointed out her inner voice. *And if you're not careful, all your lies and half-truths are going to come back to haunt you.*

It was a chilling thought, but Robyn didn't have time to dwell on it. She had a three o'clock meeting in Guadalajara and couldn't afford to miss her flight. "I have to go."

"Drink plenty of fluids and get some rest. Is it okay if I call you later?"

"I'd like that. Thanks, Sean. Bye for now."

Robyn hung up the phone, zipped up her Louis Vuitton carry-on bag and exited her suite. She felt horrible for lying to Sean, guilty about canceling their plans at the last minute, but she had a job to do, and she wouldn't let her feelings for him stand in the way.

Chapter 12

At two o'clock, when Robyn walked out of the Don Miguel Hidalgo y Costilla International Airport, a black Mercedes-Benz limousine was waiting for her at the curb. The female driver, clad in a tight navy-blue uniform, was holding a piece of paper bearing Robyn's full name and smiled in greeting as she approached. "Welcome to Guadalajara, Ms. Henderson," the brunette said with a heavy Spanish accent. "It is my pleasure to drive you to the Salazar villa this afternoon."

"*Gracias.*" Seconds later, Robyn was sitting in the backseat of the limousine, enjoying a complimentary glass of wine. And, boy, did she need it. It had been a mad dash getting to LAX during midday traffic, and if not for a kindly TSA agent, she would have missed her flight.

Robyn wanted to call Sean to check in with him but thought better of it. She was supposed to be at home resting, not cruising through the streets of Guadalajara in a stretch limo, and she didn't want to have to lie to him again about her whereabouts.

Sipping her zinfandel, she sat back comfortably in her seat and crossed her legs. Having never been to the city before, Robyn was surprised to see dozens of American stores, boutiques and restaurants. Known as "The Pearl of the West," Guadalajara's deep colonial roots and old-world charm were evident across the city, and the historic buildings were an architect's dream.

Robyn wondered if she'd have time to do some sight-seeing before her eight o'clock flight that evening and made up her mind to check out the Guadalajara Cathedral and Degollado Theater once her meeting with Enrique wrapped up. The traffic was light, and just as Robyn opened her file folder to review the notes for her presentation, the limousine slowed to a stop.

"We're here. Ms. Henderson," the driver said. "This is the Salazar estate."

Two burly Mexican men opened the wrought-iron gates and nodded at the limo driver. The grounds were spacious, filled with towering palm trees, pretty gardens and elaborate stone statues. To her surprise, Enrique was standing in front of the villa, talking on his cell phone, but the moment he saw the limousine, he ended his call and jogged down the steps.

Robyn's mouth dried, and her hands trembled. It was the moment of truth. Her time to shine, to convince Enrique that the Belleza was *the* place for his birthday bash.

To calm her nerves, she took a deep breath, then downed the rest of her wine. She'd met Enrique before—at a pre-Oscar party at the Belleza last year—and hoped this time he wouldn't flirt with her, because she wasn't in

Guadalajara to make a love connection; she was there to score the biggest contract of her career. With that thought in mind, Robyn stepped out of the limousine, adjusted her fitted Christian Dior suit and greeted Enrique with a dazzling smile.

"It's great to see you again, Robyn. I'm thrilled to have you here at my villa."

To impress him, she replied in Spanish and laughed when he kissed her excitedly on both cheeks. Robyn gave Enrique the once-over, studied him closely and decided he wasn't sick.

Panic churned in her stomach, and the truth hit her like a slap in the face. She'd been set up. Again. First, the South African businessman, and now, Enrique. Kim had tricked her, so she was stuck in Guadalajara for the rest of the day. Did he think this was a date? Was that why he was talking to her in a silky, smooth voice and tenderly caressing her forearm?

"Let me show you around." Enrique rested a hand on her lower back. "This villa used to belong to my great-great grandfather, and I inherited it when I turned nineteen."

After a tour of the grounds, they retired inside the villa for cocktails and appetizers. Robyn entered the living room and decided it was the most beautiful space she'd ever seen. It was an explosion of color—vivid reds, oranges and yellows—twice the size of her condo and filled with gleaming marble, elaborate chandeliers and plush furniture.

Robyn was sitting on the couch, plotting how to get even with Kim, when Enrique turned to her and said, "Tell me your vision for my birthday bash."

His words puzzled her, "Tell you my vision for your birthday bash?"

"Yes, of course. That's why you're here, right?" Mischief filled his eyes, and a grin tickled his lips. "Unless you dropped everything and flew over fifteen hundred miles to ask me out on a date. If that's the case my answer is hell yes!"

Robyn laughed. It turned out she was wrong. Kim hadn't set her up after all. Relieved, she crossed her legs and clasped her hands around her knees. "Let's get down to business, shall we? I have tons of great ideas, and I'm anxious to share them with you."

Robyn spoke with passion and excitement as she gave her presentation, and she could tell by the expression on Enrique's face that he was impressed. Straightening in his chair, he stared at her intensely, as if he was hanging on to her every word.

"I love the *Godfather* theme, and I think guests will enjoy Beyoncé's performance, but the party needs to be flashier, more dynamic." To emphasize his point, Enrique gestured with his hands as he spoke in rapid-fire Spanish. "Money's no object, so think big. Think huge."

Robyn scoffed inwardly but hid her true feelings behind a polite smile. Was he kidding? she thought, disappointed by his response. What could be bigger than gourmet food, a fireworks display and a performance by the biggest pop star on the planet?

"I got it!" Enrique snapped his fingers and flashed a triumphant grin, one that showcased every pearly white tooth. "The showgirls will pop out of my birthday cake, do a ten-minute routine draped all over my lap, then pose with guests from inside the cake. Brilliant, huh?"

No, it was tacky and cliché, and there was no way in

hell Kim would ever go for it. But Robyn couldn't tell Enrique the truth, not without offending him, so she nodded and pretended to write his suggestions down on her notepad. "I'll speak to our executive chef and get back to you."

"Does Sean still work at the Belleza?" Enrique picked up his glass tumbler and took a swig of his drink. "I heard from an acquaintance that he quit the resort months ago, but when I asked Kim this morning, she insisted it was nothing but a crazy rumor."

Robyn avoided Enrique's pointed stare. Kim's words came back to her, blared in her head like a siren. *If he finds out Sean isn't the executive chef of The Pearl anymore, he might take his business elsewhere, and we can't afford to lose this contract to one of our competitors.*

Robyn felt a lump in her throat, and her mouth was painfully dry, but she forced her lips to move. "Of course Sean works at the resort. It's a family-run business, and everyone's committed to—"

Hearing footsteps behind her, Robyn glanced over her shoulder. A gasp fell from her mouth. *No, no, it can't be! I must be dreaming!* But the image remained. It was Sean. He was standing in the doorway, scowling at her, and anger blazed like fire in his soulful brown eyes.

Silence engulfed the room. The air was thick with tension, so suffocating Robyn couldn't breathe. A cold chill whipped through her body, but her skin was scalding hot. "Sean, what are you doing here?"

Sean shook his head. "You first. You told me you were sick, but that's obviously a lie, because you look gorgeous."

"I second that!" Enrique said with a wink and a smile.

"Can someone please tell me what's going on?" Robyn asked, trying not to let her nervousness show despite the quiver in her voice. Seeing Sean unnerved her, left her feeling scared and confused. Her thoughts were scattered all over the map. Sean's strong, citrus cologne tickled her nose, as well as the space between her legs. Robyn told herself to quit staring at him, but she couldn't help herself. Sean looked all kinds of sexy in his baby-blue shirt, tan shorts and leather sandals, and if that wasn't bad enough, masculinity and sensuality oozed from his pores. Her hands itched to touch him, to stoke his fine, fit physique, so she buried them in her lap and stayed put on the couch. "Sean, what are you doing here?"

"Shortly after you called and canceled our plans, Enrique phoned to discuss the menu for his birthday party, and we got to talking." His expression darkened, and he folded his arms rigidly across his chest. "When Enrique told me about your three o'clock meeting, I hopped on the next flight, and here I am."

Robyn hung her head, slid down farther in her seat. Feeling guilty, like a criminal on top of the FBI's Most Wanted list, she swallowed hard and wiped her damp palms along the side of her white pencil skirt.

"I don't mean to be rude, but we need to finalize the plans for my birthday bash," Enrique said, glancing discreetly at his Rolex watch. "It's all decided then. Robyn, you'll plan the event, and Sean and his staff at the SP Grill will do all the cooking. We'll have it here, at my villa, so you'll need to order dozens of tents, tables and—"

Robyn stopped him. "I thought you were having your birthday bash at the Belleza Resort."

"And I thought Sean was still the executive chef at

The Pearl." His gaze was strong, and his anger evident. "You and Kim lied to me, and that's not cool, but since Sean assures me you're the best event planner in the business, I'm going to let it slide this one time."

"You're right," Robyn replied. "I was wrong, and I'm sorry, but I can't plan your party. You'll have to find someone else because I only do business on behalf of the Belleza Resort."

Enrique's eyebrows drew together as if he didn't understand. "I'll give you a hefty signing bonus *and* personally introduce you to my celebrity friends during the party. How does that sound?"

"I can't." Robyn smiled to prove there were no hard feelings. Enrique obviously wasn't used to hearing the word no, but it didn't matter how much money he threw at her, she wasn't turning her back on Kim or the Belleza Resort. "It was great seeing you again, Enrique. Thank you for your hospitality and for welcoming me into your lovely home."

Enrique and Sean exchanged a bewildered look.

"How much will it take to change your mind?" Enrique asked. "Five grand? Ten?"

"My loyalty isn't for sale. Now, if you'll excuse me, I have a flight to catch." Robyn stood, grabbed her purse, and exited the living room with her head held high. She didn't remember how to get back to the foyer, but she marched briskly down the hall as if she knew where she was going. Robyn had to get the hell away from Sean, and the quicker the better.

Needing a moment to catch her breath and gather her thoughts, Robyn ducked into the bathroom she saw at the end of the hallway. Like the rest of the villa the space was lavish, with marble sinks and the largest bathtub Robyn had ever seen.

Pacing, her heart pounding out of control, she replayed her meeting with Enrique in her head. Damn Sean. Why couldn't he have just stayed in LA, where he belonged? Why did he have to come to Guadalajara and ruin everything?

You're wrong for lying to him, said that inner voice she wished she could silence.

But that doesn't give him the right to stick his nose in my business.

Robyn inhaled deeply, allowed the lavender scent in the air to calm her down. Realizing she couldn't spend the rest of the day holed up in the bathroom, she grabbed her purse and yanked open the door. Robyn was shocked to see Sean standing in the hallway. Rather than show her trepidation, she hitched a hand to her hip. "What do you want?"

"You." He captured her around the waist and crushed his lips to her mouth with a savage intensity.

In a blink, Robyn was back inside the bathroom, flat against the closed door, kissing him back with everything she had. He tasted great, like fine wine, and teased her tongue with the tip of his own. His hands were under her skirt, squeezing her ass, stroking her thighs, and everything about the kiss was sensuous, hot and erotically charged.

Robyn wanted to push Sean away, wanted to yell at him for disrespecting her in front of a potential client, but she couldn't get the words out of her mouth. The truth was she wanted him, craved him, needed him like her next breath. She was filled with an intoxicating blend of hunger, and lust and knew there was no turning back when Sean yanked down her panties and rubbed his erection against her sex. He tickled her curls, then slid a finger between her legs. His pace was so fast and furious Robyn couldn't catch her breath. But first she had to apologize to Sean.

"I'm sorry I lied to you," she said, panting her words. "It was wrong."

"You're damn right it was. What were you thinking?"

"I didn't want you to be mad at me."

"Don't you ever lie to me again," he growled, his gaze locked in on her face. "We'll never have a healthy relationship if you keep secrets from me, Robyn. I always want you to be straight-up and honest with me, no matter what. Understood?"

Robyn nodded, almost wept tears of joy when his mouth reclaimed hers. Did it ever taste good. Better than chocolate. Sweeter, too. He stroked her arms and hips, excited her with each urgent caress.

"I don't believe in playing games," Sean said, reaching out and brushing a strand of hair away from her face. "Either you want to be with me, or you don't. It's your choice, and if you decide I'm not the right man for you, I'll walk out that door and out of your life forever."

His words were shocking, a painful blow. Not seeing him for the past eight months had been agonizing, and not a day went by that Robyn didn't think about him or long to be with him. "I want you, Sean, but we can't do this. Not here," she said. "What if Enrique hears us? I'd never be able to look him in the eye again."

"He won't," Sean promised, massaging her breasts. "The game's on, and he's the biggest Real Madrid fan ever, so there's no way in hell he's looking for us."

Ignoring her doubts and the voice inside her head

screaming at her to stop, Robyn unbuttoned his shorts, yanked down the zipper and slid a hand inside his boxer briefs. And there it was. His erection. Long, thick and standing attention to greet her. She hungrily licked her lips.

Robyn recognized what she was doing was reckless and irresponsible, but she wanted Sean, and in that moment, nothing else mattered. She needed Sean the way she needed sustenance. She kissed him ferociously, as if she was starving and he was lunch. And he was, without a doubt, the best thing she'd ever tasted. They hadn't made love in days, and Robyn didn't think she could survive another minute without him.

Hopping up on the counter, she pulled him to her and clamped her legs possessively around his waist. Seconds later, he was inside her, thrusting and pumping his hips. Feeling him between her legs, moving sensually against her was the greatest feeling in the world. They weren't making love, they were having sex, and Robyn loved every minute of it. It was the first time she'd had sex without her mind and heart getting in the way. And it was incredible.

Robyn loved his technique, couldn't get enough of him, wanted and needed more. She bucked hard against him, rotated her hips. Moans escaped from her mouth, ricocheted around the bathroom walls. Out of her mind with desire, she clawed at his back, dug her fingernails into his shoulders, gripped his ass, pulling him closer, deeper inside her.

Robyn felt out of it, at a complete loss of control, and buried her face in his chest to stifle her screams. It was in that moment, making love to Sean, that Robyn realized the truth: this was about more than just sex. She loved him, mind, body and soul, with every fiber of her being. Just then the climax slammed into her, and she cried out, a groan that exploded out of her mouth. She rode it until spent.

"I hope we're making love like that in twenty years, because that was incredible."

Stunned by his words, she raised her head and met his gaze. *You want a future with me?*

"Baby, are you okay?"

"Of course," she said with a dreamy smile. Her heart was overcome with love, full of joy, but she kept her feelings to herself. Robyn didn't want to scare him off or ruin the moment by getting emotional. "Sean, that was amazing. I haven't felt this good in years."

"Way to stroke a guy's ego. That's just what I wanted to hear."

Laughing, they shared a kiss and held each other tight.

"I'd better get up and pull myself together. My flight's at eight o'clock, and I can't afford to miss it." Robyn stood, gripped the counter to steady her balance and faced the mirror. At the sight of her disheveled reflection, her eyes widened in alarm. "Goodness gracious. I look a mess!"

"That's impossible. You can never look anything but beautiful."

Robyn fixed her business suit and smoothed her hands over her tangled, tousled hair.

"This is turning out to be one hell of a day," Sean said, coming up behind her and wrapping his arms around her waist. "Flying to Guadalajara was the best decision I ever made."

Turning toward him, Robyn tasted his lips, tried to

communicate everything that was in her heart through her deep, passionate kiss. "Sorry again for canceling on you, but Kim sprang this trip on me at the last minute, and I couldn't say no."

"Why is that? You have no problem saying no to me, and I'm supposed to be your man."

He spoke in a quiet voice, a tone Robyn had never heard him use before, and for some strange reason, she felt guilty, as if she'd done something wrong. She'd apologized, and they'd had a hot, explosive quickie, but something was definitely bothering him. The truth came to her, caused her mouth to dry and her heartbeat to speed up. They'd had unprotected sex—something Robyn had never done before. Was Sean thinking about the consequences of their impulsive actions? To put his fears to rest, Robyn told him, "I'm on the pill, Sean. Don't worry. I won't get pregnant."

A grin came to his lips. "Who's worried? I'd love to get married and start a family."

You would? Seriously? For real?

"Baby, I love you," he whispered, taking her in his arms. He held her close, right up to his chest. "And I couldn't imagine anything better than having a life with you."

Robyn was speechless, couldn't do anything but stare at Sean. She wanted to return the sentiment, but she couldn't bring herself to say the words. Not because she didn't share his feelings, but because the first and only time she'd said "I love you," she'd had her heart broken. And if Sean hurt her the way her college sweetheart had, Robyn knew she'd never be able to recover.

Chapter 13

"What do you want to do tonight?" Sean asked, resting his water glass on the patio table. "Hang out at the Santa Monica Pier or go dancing at Lure?"

"Neither." Robyn kicked off her high-heeled white sandals and joined Sean on the wicker sofa overlooking the infinity pool. She loved the LA nightlife and enjoyed getting dolled up for a night out on the town, but she didn't want to compete with Hollywood starlets for his attention. "I don't want to go anywhere. I want to stay here with you at your house and watch the sunset."

"And have homemade brownies, right?"

"You know it," Robyn said with a laugh. "What can I say? I love good food."

"Isn't that the truth? I still can't believe you ate two entrées at La Tequila last night."

"That's what you get for making me miss lunch."

Yesterday, after leaving Enrique's villa, they'd headed for the city center and spent the rest of the day hanging out in downtown Guadalajara. They'd taken a two-hour sightseeing tour, then strolled hand in hand through the market, snapping pictures, buying souvenirs and sampling the local cuisine. They'd shared kisses and confidences and laughs as they'd wandered from one noisy booth to the next.

Hours later, they'd had dinner at the best Mexican restaurant in the country. As Robyn was eating, she'd spotted a mariachi band enter the dining room and had been shocked when the group stopped at her table. Dressed in traditional clothes, they'd sung with excitement and strummed their instruments with dramatic flair. They'd added her name to their songs and gazed at her longingly as if they were overcome with love. Their performance had been loud and over-the-top, but Robyn had loved every raucous minute of it.

They'd returned to LA that morning, having changed her scheduled flight, but instead of returning to the resort, Robyn had gone home with Sean. From his Jaguar, she'd called and touched base with Kim. Kim was disappointed they'd lost the Salazar contract, but she'd thanked Robyn for her efforts. She'd asked Kim for another day off, and thankfully she'd agreed. Robyn had also had a lengthy conversation with Charlene about the Rabinowitz anniversary party on Saturday night. Everything was coming together perfectly, just as she'd envisioned, and Robyn was glad she could count on Charlene to keep on top of things in her absence.

"I love being out here. It's so peaceful and relaxing."

"Me, too," Robyn said, admiring the breathtaking view. "I'm having a great time."

"Of course you are. You're with me."

He kissed her, and she melted into his arms. Tilting her head to the right, she leaned into him, lovingly caressed his face. His hands were on her, too, stroking her shoulders and hips, grabbing her behind. Warmth flushed her skin, and shivers danced down her spine.

Robyn felt dizzy, out of it, as if her mind was no longer connected to her body. She ached for his touch, could almost feel him between her legs and "accidently" brushed her fingers against his groin. Yup, just as she thought: his erection was rock hard and standing at attention. "Someone's happy to see me," she teased, wiggling her eyebrows suggestively.

"Woman, you better slow your roll before I strip you naked and do you right here."

Robyn giggled and snuggled against him. They'd cooked dinner in his kitchen, eaten by candlelight, then grabbed a bottle of wine and retired to the patio. It was a gorgeous night, breezy and warm, and the sky was painted a magnificent shade of pink. Lights twinkled in the distance, made Tinsel Town look as beautiful as a postcard.

Resting her head on his chest, she closed her eyes and inhaled his spicy aftershave. The last twenty-four hours had been incredible, the most fun she'd had in years, and Robyn didn't want their time together to end. Sean had a way of making her forget everything, and for the first time in her life, she was doing just that, living in the moment with the man she loved.

The word reverberated around her mind, echoed through the four chambers of her heart. It was true. Robyn adored Sean, loved everything about him. Raising her eyes to his face, she returned his smile. *God, I*

*love when he holds me like this. There's no greater feel-
ing in the world.*

Robyn thought about their relationship, reflected on
how close they'd become in the past weeks, how tight
their bond was. He treated her like a queen, as if she
was all that mattered, and he was always doing things
to make her smile. That alone made him stand out from
every other guy she'd met in the past. Robyn could count
on one hand how many dates she'd been on since moving to the Belleza, and no one could compete with Sean.
His parents had obviously raised him right, because he
was a gentleman in every sense of the word, and the most
thoughtful, compassionate man she'd ever met.

"I'm making you dinner before Ryan's show on Sun-
day night, so meet me at the restaurant at six o'clock."
A grin brightened his eyes. "And don't be late, because
I have a special surprise for you."

"Sean, I can't go with you to the show."

"Why? Because you're scared of someone seeing us
together?"

Robyn gulped a breath of fresh air. He knew how she
felt and why. But tonight she didn't want to argue with
Sean, not after the romantic, candlelit dinner they'd had.
She made up her mind to keep the peace, no matter what.

"I'm tired of sneaking around." His eyes darkened, and
his lips curled into a sneer. "Are we ever going to date
like other couples, or is this as good as it gets?"

To lighten the mood, Robyn flashed a cheeky smile.
"We're just having fun, remember?"

"Fun?" Sean repeated, wrinkling his nose. "Naw,
baby, I'm in this for the long haul."

Robyn parted her lips but tripped over her tongue
when she tried to speak.

"What do I have to do to prove my love to you?" He leaned back in his chair and stroked the length of his jaw. "Do you want to elope? Would that put your doubts to rest once and for all if we tied the knot in Las Vegas?"

"That's crazy. We'd probably be divorced within the year."

Sean cocked his head to the left, stared at her so intently her skin flushed with heat.

"Is this about your parents?"

Robyn's smile vanished, and her eyes narrowed. "What are you talking about?"

"Just because your parents divorced doesn't mean you can't have a successful marriage."

"My reluctance to settle down has nothing to do with my parents and everything to do with my horrible track record with men, starting with my college sweetheart," she blurted out.

"Did he break your heart?"

Over and over and over again, but who's counting?

Robyn opened her mouth, but then she realized she didn't know what to say and slammed it shut. Only Kim and Gabby knew what had happened with her college sweetheart, Gary Edmonds, but she wanted to open up to Sean, felt compelled to tell him the truth. "Gary and I had a rocky relationship from the start, but in spite of our differences, we dated off and on my first two years of college."

"Did you think he was the one?"

"Yes, of course. He was my first love and I thought we'd be together forever." Gazing out at the night sky, she allowed her thoughts to wander, to return to her junior year. Her pulse quickened, and perspiration soaked her skin. She was sweating like a tourist lost in the hood and her heart was beating so fast she feared it would explode out of her chest. "I found out I was pregnant just weeks after my twentieth birthday, and my whole world fell apart."

His pupils dilated, and his jaw fell slack. "I had no idea."

"No one did. Only Kim and Gabby, and I swore them to secrecy."

"Was your ex supportive? Was he excited about the baby?"

"I thought he was…" Robyn hesitated, waited for the room to stop spinning. She felt a rush of emotion and bit the inside of her cheek to keep her tears at bay. Opening up about her past was harder than she thought, but since she wanted him to understand her better, she soldiered on. "Gary proposed on the spot and promised to be there for me and the baby."

"Sounds like a stand-up guy."

"He wasn't. It was all an act." An acrid taste filled her mouth, and Robyn feared she was going to be sick. It had been eight years since her ex had abandoned her, but his betrayal still stung. "Gary was a no-show at my doctor's appointment the next day, and he literally fell of the face of the earth. A month later, I found out through his roommates that he'd transferred to another school."

"He got cold feet."

"So? I was scared, too," she argued. "I needed his support, not lies and empty promises."

"I'm not making excuses for him, Robyn. I'm just giving you a male perspective. I used to be a young, dumb, twenty-year-old, so I can sympathize with your ex-boyfriend."

Scared she'd burst into tears, she looked away. Touching her throat, she fiddled with the pendant hanging on her diamond chain. Her pregnancy had changed her and her views about the opposite sex, made her believe men couldn't be trusted. She'd hardened her heart and refused to let anyone get close to her, though many had tried. And to this day, Robyn couldn't look at her dad without feeling resentful. He'd abandoned her when she needed him most, and after all these years her heart still ached. Her mother implored her to forgive, so did Kim and Gabby, but her pain was deep, and for once, Robyn wanted her dad to reach out to her.

"Did you give the baby up for adoption?"

Robyn knew the question was coming, had been dreading it and now struggled with her words. "There is no baby," she said, feeling a lump form in her throat. She took a moment to gather herself and pushed the truth out of her mouth. "I had a miscarriage at thirteen weeks."

Sean stared deep into her eyes. "I wish I had known. I would have done something to help."

"I survived. I had my studies, my internship at Elite Catering to keep me busy, and Kim and Gabby, of course. They were there for me during my darkest times, when I felt lost and alone, and I'll always love them for being true friends."

"I'm glad they were there for you. That makes me happy."

"Your sister's an amazing person, and I'll always be in her debt."

"Thank you for telling me about your past. I know it couldn't have been easy for you to open up like that." His eyes were sad, but he spoke in a soft, soothing voice, one that calmed her nerves. "I feel like I know you better now, and that's a very good thing."

"Really? You think so?"

"Absolutely. Now I know why you won't fully commit to me and why you're keeping me at arm's length." Sean cupped her chin in his hand and forced her to meet his gaze. "You're scared of history repeating itself. But you have nothing to worry about. I'll never do anything to hurt you or betray your trust."

His words hit home, made her reflect on her past heartbreak. Robyn realized everything Sean had said was true. She *was* scared of being hurt and worried one day he'd get bored with her and move on to the next girl. He'd broken hearts before, and she feared it was just a matter of time before he dropped her for someone else. To quiet her doubts, she asked the question that had been plaguing her thoughts for weeks. "Is there a chance you and Trina will get back together?"

"Not a chance in hell."

Robyn sighed in relief and smiled when he playfully nuzzled his nose against hers.

"Baby, you're my heart, and I'll cherish you forever."

Robyn exhaled, told herself not to get caught up in the moment. She was careful with her words, tried to be considerate of his feelings. "We haven't been dating long, and I think it's important we take our time, because the last thing I want to do is ruin our friendship—"

Hearing her cell phone ring, Robyn stopped speaking. She picked it up and read the number on the screen. It was Kim, but before she could answer, Sean plucked it out of her hand and held it high in the air.

"Sean, give me back my phone. It's Kim, and she'll worry if I don't answer."

"You're officially off the clock, so quit thinking about the resort."

As usual, Sean was right. She should be relaxing, not fretting about work, but when her cell stopped ringing and started up again seconds later Robyn demanded her phone back. She hadn't spoken to Kim in hours, and she felt guilty for not responding to her numerous text messages. "I'll make it quick. I promise."

Sean looked annoyed, as if he wanted to argue, but he reluctantly handed over her cell phone. "I'm going to grab dessert, but you'd better be off the phone when I get back, or else."

"Baby, don't worry, I will," she said, winking at him. "Nothing is more important to me than spending time with you, and when you get back, it's on!"

His eyes brightened, and a grin claimed his lips. "Good answer," he whispered, his voice a husky growl. "I was hoping you'd say that." Sean leaned in and smothered her mouth with his own. The kiss aroused her body, made Robyn feel euphoric, as if she was walking on air. Her mind went blank. She forgot all about Kim and focused her attention on pleasing her man.

Time passed with no end in sight to the kiss. They talked dirty, pawed at each other's clothes, laughed and played. Robyn loved what he was doing with his tongue, wished it was buried deep between her legs. His lips were an aphrodisiac, his hands were instruments of pleasure, and his voice was a turn-on.

Robyn heard her cell phone ringing, knew it was Kim calling back and reluctantly ended the kiss. It had better be important or Robyn was going to give her an earful.

"You have five minutes and not a second more."

Sean strode into the house, leaving Robyn on the settee. Fanning her face, she blew out a deep breath and put her cell to her ear. "Hey, girl, what's up?"

"I've been calling you for the last ten minutes. Why didn't you answer?"

Robyn frowned, wondered what was wrong with Kim. She sounded upset, as if she was crying. "Sorry about that. I was in the middle of something. Is everything okay?"

"There's been…an accident." Her voice quivered, cracked with emotion, and a bitter sob escaped her throat. "Jonah got hurt."

"What do you mean, there's been an accident? What happened? Where's Jonah now? Can I talk to him?" Robyn knew she was rambling, speaking faster than an auctioneer, but Jonah was important to her, and she had to get to the bottom of things. The elderly bartender cared about her—and the rest of the Belleza staff—and Robyn loved him like a father.

"Jonah was struck by some lighting set up for the Rabinowitz party," Kim said.

Robyn sat up straight, pressed the phone closer to her ear. "Where is he now?"

Silence filled the line, lasted so long Robyn repeated the question.

"He's in critical condition at the Belleza Medical Center." Kim sniffed. "And the doctors don't think he's going to make it."

Sean opened the walk-in pantry, flipped on the lights and searched the wine rack for a bottle of 1989 zinfandel. It was Robyn's favorite wine, and he'd bought it specifically for her. He heard the patio doors slide open and knew why his lady love was hot on his heels. "Don't worry. I didn't forget the brownies," he joked with a laugh. "The container's on the counter. Go ahead and help yourself, but save some for me."

"I have to leave."

Sean abandoned his search and exited the pantry. He took one look at Robyn and knew she'd been crying. Her bottom lip was trembling, mascara stained her cheeks, and her shoulders were hunched in despair. "Baby, what's wrong?"

"There was an accident at the resort."

Sean crossed the room and gathered her in his arms. As she recounted her conversation with Kim, her voice faltered and she burst into tears. He held her close to his chest, assured her everything was going to be all right, tenderly stroked her hair and neck.

"Jonah's a fighter," he said, refusing to believe his favorite bartender had been gravely injured that afternoon. "He'll pull through this. I know it. We have to have faith."

"And if he doesn't?"

"Don't think like that. Jonah's one of the strongest people I know."

Robyn slowly nodded her head, seemed to draw strength from his words, and wiped her eyes with her fingertips. "Thanks for the pep talk. I needed that."

"I'll grab my cell from the bedroom, then we'll head to the hospital."

"I didn't want to inconvenience you, so I called a cab. It'll be here soon."

"No worries. Just cancel it from my car." Sean glanced at his Rolex watch. "Visiting hours probably ended at eight, but I'd still like to look in on Jonah, even if it's just for a few minutes."

"We can't go to the hospital together. Your parents are

there, and so are Kim, Gabby, their fiancés and a half-dozen resort employees."

"I don't give a damn who's there," he said, dropping his arms from around her waist. "I consider Jonah family, and I deserve to be at the hospital just as much as anyone else."

"I never said you shouldn't go. I said *I* couldn't go with you."

Sean saw the stress lines on Robyn's face, heard the anger in her voice and struggled to keep his temper in check. If anyone should be mad, it should be him, not her. Her refusal to publicly acknowledge their relationship was evidence that she was ashamed of it, ashamed of him. In her eyes, he wasn't good enough, and Sean feared that would never change. *Will Kim and the resort always come first? Will I ever be a priority, or will I always be an afterthought?*

Robyn held firm. "This isn't the right time to go public with our relationship."

"You've been saying that for weeks," he argued, throwing his hands up in the air in frustration. Sean needed to know where he stood with Robyn, and he asked her point-blank. "Either you want to be with me or you don't. Which one is it?"

"Sean, I care about you, and I want us to be together—"

"Then prove it. Come with me to the hospital."

A fleeting look of remorse flickered across her face. "You know why I can't."

"Because you're ashamed of me, right?"

"No, of course not, but I need to be there for Kim."

"Did you ever stop to think about how *I* feel?" he asked, jabbing a finger at his chest. "I love Jonah, too, and I could use your support right now, but I guess that's too much to ask. Kim and the Belleza are obviously all you care about, and that will never change."

Robyn started to speak, to argue that he was wrong, but he cut her off at her first word.

"Damn, I feel like such a fool. From day one, you made it clear you'd never commit to me, but I didn't believe you. I figured I could change your mind." Sean hung his head, raked a hand through his hair and along the back of his neck. "I thought you'd fall for me, and we'd live happily ever after. Stupid, huh?"

"Don't make me out to be the bad guy in this."

"I never said you were."

"For fourteen years you never gave me a second glance, and now all of a sudden, you want to be my man?" Her tone was rife with accusation and suspicion, sharper than the tip of a sword. "If I wasn't Kim's best friend, you wouldn't be pursuing me so hard."

"What are you talking about? You're not making any sense."

"I'm not stupid, Sean. I know what you're doing, so don't pretend to be the victim."

Four-letter words exploded out of his mouth, ricocheted around the room like bullets. Her accusations cut him to the quick, but Sean told himself Robyn didn't mean it, couldn't mean it. Not after everything they'd been through.

"Hooking up with me is the perfect way to hurt Kim, isn't it?"

"Is that what you think? That I'm using you to get back at my sister?" Sean scoffed, shook his head in disbelief. What a sick twist of fate. He'd finally found the woman of his dreams, the person he wanted to spend the rest of his life with, but she didn't trust him. How screwed up was that? He'd been straight-up with Robyn from the beginning, but it wasn't good enough. He wasn't good enough.

"I've said this before, but it obviously bears repeating. My feelings for you have nothing to do with Kim and everything to do with the captivating, vivacious woman you are."

Robyn cast her eyes away, chose to look at the floor instead of at him, and his heart deflated like a popped balloon. The longer the silence lasted, the more hopeless he felt, but he had to speak his mind. "Robyn, I love spending time with you, but I'm through sneaking around. It's juvenile and silly and we're better than that."

"We wouldn't have to sneak around if you'd made amends with your family like I asked you to." Her face softened, and she offered her cell phone, touched his forearm with it. "Sean, it isn't too late. You can do it now. Call Kim and make things right."

Sean took a deep breath, but it didn't calm his nerves. He was done. Finished. Sick and tired of having the same argument over and over again. He'd had enough of people telling him what to do—Trina demanding he propose, his mother begging him to make peace with his dad, Robyn imploring him to reach out to Kim. It was all too much, more than any man could take. "I'll make amends with my family as soon as *you* make amends with yours."

Her nose twitched, and her bottom lip trembled. "It's not the same thing."

"Yes, it is," he argued. "How can you nag me about making amends with my family when you haven't spoken to your dad in years?"

"I've tried, but he won't talk to me," she shouted, her voice quivering uncontrollably. Tears spilled down her cheeks, splashed onto her sundress like raindrops. "I called him on Father's Day, and he hung up the phone on me…his only daughter…"

Guilt stabbed his heart, troubled his conscience. He'd gone too far, said too much. Her pain was evident, written all over her face, and Sean felt like an ass for hurting her feelings. Filled with remorse, he touched a hand to her waist.

She recoiled in disgust, as if his hand was dirty, and wiped the tears coursing furiously down her cheeks. "Don't even *think* of touching me."

"Robyn, I'm sorry," he said, meaning it from the bottom of his heart. "I shouldn't have said that. Your relationship with your father is none of my business."

A light shone in the window, and a car horn blared, drawing his attention to the foyer.

"You know what, Sean? Sometimes you can be a real jerk, and now I see why you're estranged from your family." Robyn snatched her purse off the counter and slung it over her shoulder. Fire blazed in her eyes as she gave voice to her anger. "Kim was right. You're selfish and petty, and you don't care about anyone but yourself."

The verbal blow knocked the wind out of him, made him feel lower than a snake. And the look on her face said it all. They were through, and there wasn't a damn thing he could do about it.

Robyn was his world, the only thing that mattered, and Sean didn't know how he was going to live without her. How had they got there? How had things turned so bad so quickly? One minute they were outside on the patio having a heart-to-heart talk about her past, and the next, they were arguing about their relationship, fighting like cats and dogs.

"I don't have time for this," Robyn said with a glance out the window. "I'm out of here."

Sean opened his mouth but couldn't think of anything to say. It wasn't in his character to beg, and although he was dying inside, he couldn't bring himself to chase after her. At a loss for words, he stood there, wishing he could take back the things he'd said. He'd never quit at anything, but he had no fight left in him, and he knew letting her go was the right thing to do.

Sadness welled up inside his chest as he watched Robyn walk out of his house and out of his life forever. He felt an acute sense of loss, like a widower standing beside a casket, and struggled to control his emotions. Robyn slammed the front door so hard his ears throbbed, and when Sean glanced out the window at the departing taxi, he realized today—not the day he'd quit the resort—was the worst day of his life.

Chapter 14

Robyn's day was off to a horrible start. She'd overslept, which resulted in her being late for a meeting with a potential client, then had a heated conversation with Mr. Rabinowitz about his anniversary party on Saturday, and if that wasn't bad enough, she'd gotten a flat tire driving to the Belleza Medical Center that afternoon, and had no choice but to pull over and change it herself.

Swallowing a yawn, Robyn crossed her legs and clasped her hands around her knees. She'd arrived at the Parker family estate ten minutes earlier with Kim and Gabby, curious as to why Mr. Parker had called an emergency meeting in the middle of the day, especially in light of everything that was going on.

Last night after leaving Sean's house, she'd picked up her car from the airport and driven straight to the hospital. There, she'd found the waiting room jam-packed with people who loved Jonah and with several pesky reporters, who'd heard about the accident at the resort. There'd been no change in his condition, and when the nursing staff had asked everyone to leave, Robyn had reluctantly returned to the resort. She'd tossed and turned in bed for hours, reliving her argument with Sean. She felt guilty for losing her temper and knew she wouldn't have peace until she apologized to Sean, but Robyn couldn't bring herself to call him. Her focus was on supporting Jonah, any way she could, and for now, that was all that mattered.

At the thought of the kindly old man with the jovial disposition, a sad smile touched Robyn's lips. On the way to the Parker estate that afternoon, she'd stopped at the hospital to visit Jonah. He was stable, but his vitals were weak, and he was unresponsive. To pass the time, she'd read him magazines, filled him in on what was happening at the Belleza, and opened up to him about Sean. Sure, he was unconscious, but putting her feelings into words was surprisingly therapeutic. By the time Robyn left the hospital two hours later, she felt less emotional about their fight and back in control of her thoughts and emotions.

Really? questioned her inner voice. *Then why did you burst into tears when you drove past Manhattan Beach? You were crying so hard you had to pull over.*

Before she could answer that personal question, Kurt Parker entered. He stood before them in the formal living room and refused a seat. Without any preamble, he got right to it. "I asked you to come here this afternoon because I wanted to pass along some sensitive information, and I couldn't risk someone at the resort overhearing our discussion."

Robyn shook off any thoughts and gave Mr. Parker her full attention. There was much to discuss, and she didn't want to miss anything. News of Jonah's freak accident at The Pearl had made all of the newspapers, and the media were accusing the resort of negligence. Worse still, there were fictitious reports about buried treasure at the resort, and the curse of the Belleza had reared its ugly head once again. Guests had been checking out of the resort by the dozens ever since the story had aired on the local news, and the front desk staff couldn't keep up with the record number of cancellations.

"I spoke to Fenton, the detective handling the case, at length this morning, and he confirmed my suspicions. Jonah's accident was no accident. Someone tampered with the lighting at The Pearl."

Robyn leaned forward in her chair, listened intently to what Mr. Parker was saying.

"I don't know if Jonah was the intended target or not, but the police believe whoever's behind the accident had help from someone on the inside, so you need to be extra cautious at the resort. Someone is out to ruin the Belleza, and until they're apprehended, no one's safe."

"Maybe we should close the resort for the time being," Ilene Parker suggested.

Kim and her dad spoke in unison. "No!"

"Not indefinitely," Mrs. Parker explained, glancing from her daughter to her husband, her eyes pleading for understanding. "Just until the police arrest the perpetrators. We can't risk someone else getting hurt—"

"Absolutely not," Kim said, adamantly shaking her head, her ponytail swishing furiously back and forth. "We're Parkers, and Parkers don't back down to anyone."

Mr. Parker beamed with pride, as if Kim had scored a hole in one on the golf course. "I couldn't have said it better myself, baby girl. We'll hire additional security and have staff implement the buddy system when traveling around the resort after dark, but as they say on Broadway, the show must go on."

Mrs. Parker balked. "Money isn't everything, Kurt. You of all people should know that."

Knowing the history of the resort, Robyn knew Mrs. Parker was referring to the difficult economic times the couple had faced decades earlier. Luckily, their hard work and sacrifice had paid off, and they'd been able to turn things around. The resort had experienced a healthy resurgence in the nineties and regained its reputation as the premier resort in California.

It was Kim who replied to her mother's remark. "Mom, I understand your concern, but closing the resort simply isn't an option. We're hosting several big events this weekend, not to mention this is our busiest time of year and by far the most profitable."

"Kim, please reconsider. I want you and the employees to be safe, and I have a feeling Jonah's accident is just the tip of the iceberg."

In spite of her outward calm, Robyn was nervous and afraid. Was Mrs. Parker right? Were things going to get worse at the resort? Could Kim be next? Could *she*?

"Do the police have any leads?" Gabby asked, addressing Mr. Parker. "Detectives interviewed me this morning, but when I asked about the investigation, they clammed up."

"Detective Fenton is confident they'll make an arrest soon and is working around the clock to track down every lead. He's headed to the SP Grill as we speak."

"The SP Grill?" Mrs. Parker repeated, raising an eyebrow. "What for?"

"To rule out Sean as a suspect."

"Kurt, that's preposterous, and you know it."

"I'm hoping for the best, Ilene, but it wouldn't be the first time he's tried to hurt us."

"Sean adores Jonah, and he'd never do anything to destroy the Belleza, so call that sour-faced detective and tell him to leave my baby the hell alone!"

Robyn cheered inwardly. *That's right, Ilene! Set him straight!* Sean couldn't have tampered with the lighting—because he'd been at home with her. But fear of being fired forced Robyn to keep that alibi to herself. She couldn't tell the Parkers the truth, but she was prepared to come clean if this Detective Fenton interviewed her.

Kim spoke up. "Mom, I don't think Sean tampered with the lighting, either, but we have to let the police do their job." She glanced at her friends. "It will be business as usual at the resort. Right, ladies?"

"Not quite, Kim. Guests have been canceling their reservations, and both restaurants were practically empty when I left the resort this afternoon," Gabby explained, her tone solemn. "From what I understand, guests have been calling, wanting to refund their tickets for the Dunham Foundation gala."

The color drained from Kim's face.

"And that's not all." Robyn wished she didn't have to be the bearer of more bad news, but she couldn't put off telling Kim about the problems in her department. "Mr. Rabinowitz read about Jonah's accident in the newspaper and is threatening to have their event at another resort."

"But we've spent tens of thousands of dollars on their anniversary party," Kim argued.

"I know, and I reminded him of our contract, but he wouldn't listen."

"If they take their business elsewhere, it will ruin our

reputation. A black-tie event for two hundred guests is a huge deal, so let's put our heads together and figure out how to fix this."

"Rabinowitz and I go way back," Mr. Parker said. "I'll call him and smooth things over."

"Thanks, Dad, but don't worry. I've got this."

Robyn was proud of Kim for not taking the easy way out. Her best friend was determined to stand on her own two feet, just like her big brother, and that was admirable.

At the thought of Sean, happy memories flooded her heart. Strolling along the beach hand in hand, cooking dinner at the SP Grill and sightseeing in Guadalajara. Tears filled her eyes, and her throat closed up. Robyn needed something cold to drink, but her vision was so blurry she couldn't see her water glass.

"Robyn, are you okay? You don't look too good."

"I'm fine," she lied, faking a polite smile. "I'm just worried about Jonah, that's all."

Nodding, her expression one of sympathy, Mrs. Parker reached over and squeezed her hand. "Be positive, Robyn. Jonah's a fighter. He'll pull through."

Robyn dropped her gaze to her lap. Sean had said the same thing last night, and remembering how loving he'd been as she'd cried in his arms brought a fresh wave of guilt. *What have I done? Why did I push him away when all he wanted to do was help?*

The phone on the end table sounded, and Mr. Parker picked it up on the second ring. As he spoke, he grimaced and hung his head. Seconds later, he dropped the phone in the cradle and rubbed at his eyes with the back of his hand.

"Dad, what is it? What's wrong?"

"That was the hospital."

Mrs. Parker touched her husband's leg. "Honey, what did the doctor say?"

"Jonah's conscious, but his vitals are weak. They suggested we go pay our final respects."

"Damn, bro, you look like hell."

"Thanks, Ryan. It's good to see you, too." Sean hugged his kid brother and clapped him hard on the shoulder. He'd called him that morning as he was leaving the Belleza Medical Center and told him about Jonah's freak accident. Ryan had cancelled his gigs for the rest of the week and hopped on the next flight to LA.

The airport was loud and crowded, but as they headed to the exit, Sean noticed several cuties making eyes at his kid brother.

Ryan was tall and handsome like their father, but more laid-back. His wire-rimmed glasses, neatly trimmed goatee and casual attire gave off a boy-next-door vibe, but his twenty-six-year-old brother liked living on the wild side, and that would never change.

Twenty minutes after arriving at LAX, Sean was back behind the wheel of his sports car, flying down the freeway. "How was your flight?"

"Great. Sat beside an Aussie beauty who's the splitting image of Rihanna."

"When are you seeing her again?"

"Tonight, if you lend me the keys to your Lambo," he said with a wink and a smile.

Sean belted out a hearty laugh, chuckled as if it was the funniest thing he'd ever heard. "Not on your life. The last time I let you drive my Lamborghini, you scratched the bumper."

"Bro, it was like that when I left the house."

"Sure, and you know nothing about all those speeding tickets, either. Right?"

Ryan wore an innocent face. "That's right, bro. Nothing at all."

The brothers shared a laugh.

"Any word on Jonah?" Ryan asked, his voice suddenly turning serious. "Is he still unconscious?"

Sean nodded, felt his grip tighten around the steering wheel. Media reports suggested someone had tampered with the lighting in The Pearl, and he was furious anyone would try to harm Jonah. He was determined to find out who the culprit was and planned to make a trip to the Belleza first thing tomorrow morning. "Jonah's pretty banged up. He has broken ribs, a punctured lung and a fractured leg."

"Poor Jonah. My heart breaks for the old guy."

"I know you're anxious to see him, but I figured we'd have lunch at the SP Grill before heading to the hospital."

Ryan licked his lips and patted his stomach. "Good call, bro. I missed your tasty cooking."

On the drive to the restaurant, the brothers talked about sports, the weather and Ryan's budding music career. It was the first time all day Sean wasn't obsessing about Robyn. His brother's outrageous stories about the Big Apple provided the perfect distraction.

"I love this song." Ryan turned up the volume on the radio and grooved to the music. "I do this Otis Redding track at the end of every set, and the audience always goes wild."

His voice was strong, and he sang with such feeling and emotion Sean almost believed he was suffering from a broken heart. He couldn't believe how much his brother's voice had matured in the last year, how silky smooth it was. Robyn was right. Ryan should be the musical guest for the grand opening celebration.

"What's for lunch?"

"Good question," Sean said, activating his Bluetooth earpiece. He called Jolene to check in with her, and when they entered the restaurant ten minutes later, Sean could smell her down-home cooking in the air. After introductions were made, Sean gave Ryan a tour of the restaurant. As they walked through the lounge, shooting the breeze and cracking jokes, Sean was reminded of the first time he'd brought Robyn there. To this day, he couldn't sit at his office desk without thinking about her hot body or hearing her loud, feverish moans in his ears.

"Your grand opening's approaching soon," Ryan said, glancing around the dining room with an appreciative expression on his face. "Are you nervous?"

Yeah, about living the rest of my life without Robyn. Sean roped his thoughts back in, cautioned himself not to go there. Robyn had made her decision, he'd made his, and there was no turning back. "I'm confident the night will be a success. Eighty-seven percent of the dining room has already been reserved, and my musical guest is going to bring the house down."

"Word? Don't keep me in suspense. Who is it?"

Sean grinned from ear-to-ear. "You."

"Me?" Ryan asked, pointing at his chest. "No way. Is this a trick? Are you punking me?"

"No. I want someone young and exciting to kick off the grand opening celebration, and I couldn't think of anyone better than you. So, what do you say? Do you want the job?"

Slanting his head to the right, his eyes narrowed in concentration, he slowly stroked the length of his chiseled jaw. "I usually charge six figures for a two-hour set, but since we're family, I'll give you a discount. Just this one time."

Sean chuckled and ruffled his brother's short dark hair. "Just don't forget to give me a shout-out when you win your first Grammy."

"You can bet on it, bro. Now can we eat?"

They sat at the bar, and Jolene appeared with an oversize tray filled with garlic mashed potatoes, collard greens, Southern-fried chicken and two ice-cold beers. "Enjoy!"

Jolene waved, then disappeared back inside the kitchen. With all the running around Sean had done that morning, he hadn't had time to eat, so he devoured his meal in seconds. Thoughts of Robyn were heavy on his mind, and he couldn't help wondering how she was doing. Through conversation with Jonah's head nurse, he'd learned that Robyn had left the Belleza Medical Center just moments before he'd arrived that morning. Try as he might, he couldn't stop thinking about her. He longed to hold her, to make love to her just one more time. Did she miss him? he wondered, feeling a heaviness in his chest. And if she did, why hadn't she called? Didn't she know he was dying a slow, agonizing death without her? Did she even care?

"I like your girl." Ryan helped himself to a butter-milk biscuit from the wicker basket and took a big bite. "She's good people and real easy on the eyes, too, bro. Nice choice."

"Jolene's not my girlfriend. She's my assistant manager and nothing more."

"I'm confused. You told me you met someone."

Sean pressed his eyes shut to block the images of

Robyn that flashed in his mind and released a deep sigh. "We're through."

"That was fast. What happened?"

"Don't ask."

"Let me guess." Ryan paused to wipe his mouth with a napkin, then dropped it on the bar. "She asked you to commit, and you dropped her like a bad habit, didn't you?"

"No, it was the other way around," he said, feeling the need to defend himself.

"Liar." Ryan reached for his beer bottle, and raised it to his lips. "You've never been serious about anyone, and you know it."

"Robyn isn't just another girl. She's smart and witty and vivacious."

Ryan choked on his beer. "Robyn Henderson? Kim's best friend?"

"The one and only."

"Holy crap. Kim must have gone ballistic when she found out you guys were dating."

"Kim doesn't know. Robyn insisted we keep our relationship a secret." Needing to vent, Sean told his brother about the argument they'd had last night. "I lost my temper, and in the heat of the moment, I said things I didn't mean."

"Kim, Gabby and Robyn have been thick as thieves since they were teens. You can't expect Robyn to throw their friendship away for you," he said, placing his empty beer bottle back down on the bar. "Furthermore, you don't have the best track record when it comes to the ladies, and Robyn was probably scared of ending up on the chopping block."

"What's that supposed to mean?"

"You're afraid of commitment."

Sean scowled and shook his head. "No, I'm not."

"Dude, who are you kidding? You've *never* been in a serious relationship, and as soon as a woman mentions the C word you cut her lose. Case in point, Trina Erickson."

"Trina isn't Robyn. They're two completely different women," he explained. "Robyn is in a league of her own, and I'm a hundred percent ready to commit to her."

"Then call and tell her that."

"I did, and she rejected me."

"Then try again, and keep trying until she takes you back."

Sean had to admit what his brother said made sense, but he couldn't conquer his doubts, couldn't ignore the voice telling him he wasn't good enough for her, that he'd always come behind Kim and the resort on her priority list. Robyn was the best thing that had ever happened to him, and he'd been a fool to let her go, but what choice did he have? Sean wanted to be number one in her life, not an afterthought. He wanted Robyn to be proud to be his girl, not embarrassed. He loved her with everything in him. He loved her enough to let her go.

"I need to find a date for Kim's wedding, or I'm going to be the odd man out," Ryan complained, drumming his fingers absently on the granite bar. "Speaking of Kim's wedding, have you bought your tuxedo yet?"

"I'm not going."

Ryan glared at him with open contempt, as if he couldn't stand to look at him, and he elbowed him hard in the ribs. "Dude, she's your sister, the only one you've got, and it'll break her heart if you're not there on her big day."

Sean opened his mouth to argue his case, but Ryan interrupted him.

"I know you're pissed about not being awarded control of the Belleza, but it's time to let it go and move on. Kim needs you and if you don't make things right, you'll lose her forever."

Fear flooded Sean's body. As he sat at the bar, contemplating his future, Robyn's words came back to him, played in his mind at a deafening pitch. *Sometimes you can be a real jerk, and now I see why you're estranged from your family. Kim was right. You're selfish and petty, and you don't care about anyone but yourself.*

Sean hung his head, stroked his freshly trimmed mustache. He had the best of everything money could buy, but what did it matter if he didn't have his family and the woman he loved more than anything in the world?

Ryan's words broke through his thoughts. "Sean, this feud has gone on long enough. It's time to reunite with our family."

He looked at his younger brother. "Maybe you're right."

"Of course I'm right." Ryan's grin was wicked and mischief gleamed in his grayish-brown eyes. "Straighten things out with Kim, then go get your girl back, because it would be a damn shame if you lost Robyn to someone who looks just like me!"

Chapter 15

God, please don't let Jonah die. I need him and so does the Belleza Resort, Robyn prayed silently, clasping Kim's and Gabby's hands as they exited the elevator on Unit Six of the Belleza Medical Center. They walked down the corridor, but the blue walls and vibrant paintings did nothing to calm her frazzled nerves.

Staring at the clock at the end of the hall, she watched the seconds tick by, praying the next wouldn't be Jonah's last. A television blared some game show inside the waiting room, nurses hustled from one end of the unit to the next, and the scent of death was so heavy in the air Robyn felt sick to her stomach.

After Kurt had received the call from Jonah's doctor he'd ended their meeting and advised everyone to go directly to the Belleza Medical Center.

Entering Jonah's private room, Robyn gathered herself and took a deep, calming breath. She was crying on the inside but plastered a bright smile on her face. She feared this would be the last visit she'd ever have with Jonah and wished Sean was with her. He was close to Jonah, and Robyn knew how much the two men loved each other. She considered calling Sean, to give him an update on Jonah's condition, but decided against it. They were finished, and the only hope she had of ever getting over him was severing all ties.

Good luck with that, said her inner voice. *You can't go five minutes without thinking about Sean, and that will never change. He is, and always will be, the love of your life.*

Robyn pushed aside her thoughts and followed her friends into the room. The blinds were drawn and the air conditioner was blowing, but perspiration drenched her skin. Monitors beeped, drawing her attention to the bed, and to her surprise, Jonah was awake. He was gazing out the window, a pensive expression on his face. He looked so vulnerable, so weak and frail, tears came to Robyn's eyes.

"It's good to see you, Jonah. How are you feeling?" Kim asked quietly.

Turning away from the window, he acknowledged her presence with a nod. His eyes were empty, and he looked defeated, as if he had no fight left in him.

"Do you need anything?" Gabby wore a small smile, gestured to the door with her hand. "Do you want me to get you something to eat from the cafeteria?"

"A rum and cola would be nice." His voice was hoarse, and talking seemed to require all his strength, but amusement colored his sunken cheeks. "And while you're at it, bring me one of your juicy steak burgers, because hospital food sucks."

The friends shared a knowing look.

Some things never changed, Robyn thought, shaking her head at the wise-cracking bartender. Jonah was in pain, but he hadn't lost his sense of humor.

"Robyn, come closer. I need to speak to you in private. It's important."

Her body froze. *Is this the end? Is this the last time we'll ever talk? Ever see each other?* Swallowing the lump in her throat, she moved to the bed and took his hand in hers. Jonah Grady was a sweet man, one of the kindest people she'd ever met, and she'd never forget all the times he'd given her advice. He was the heart and soul of the Belleza Resort, and things wouldn't be the same without him.

"Have you reconciled with Sean?" Jonah asked, speaking only loud enough for her to hear. "Did you apologize for pushing him away and finally profess your love?"

A gasp fell from her mouth, and the room flipped upside down on its head. Robyn was stunned. How could Jonah possibly know about her secret relationship with Sean? He'd been unconscious when she'd spilled her guts that afternoon, right? Straining to hear him, she leaned in close and concentrated on what he was saying.

"The bond between you and Sean has existed for years, but he didn't want to ruin your friendship by confessing his true feelings. He spent many nights at the bar after work, talking my ear off about you, you know."

He had? She'd had no idea.

"I know you're committed to your career, but you have to find a way to have Sean *and* the Belleza. You're destined to be together, and I know in my heart he'll take good care of you. I might be an old man, but I know a thing or two about love."

Robyn moved even closer, soaked up his words of wisdom. As Jonah spoke, gently admonishing her about the affairs of the heart, Robyn knew what she had to do. Being without Sean, not having him in her life was a terrifying concept, and Robyn didn't want him to be the one who got away. He made her feel safe, took care of her, never let a day go by without telling her she was beautiful and smart and special. Sean understood her, believed in her and, most important, loved her. And, thanks to Jonah, she'd realized the errors of her ways.

"There is nothing worth more than love." Wearing a sad smile, he patted her hand. "Always remember that."

Sniffling, she fervently nodded her head. "I will. I promise."

"I wasted years of my life chasing rainbows or, more accurately, hidden treasures…"

For the second time in minutes, Robyn was speechless. She was stunned by what Jonah whispered in her ear. She didn't know whether to believe him or not and wondered if his confession was the truth or just the ramblings of a dying man. The only thing Robyn knew for sure was that she had to reconcile with Sean before it was too late. She sensed Kim and Gabby beside her, could hear their soft cries and hugged them to her side to comfort them.

"We love you, Jonah," they said in unison.

"I love you girls, too. Keep in mind what's really important in life…" His eyelids grew heavy, his voice trailed off, and his arms fell limply at his sides.

Seconds later, nurses burst into the room and worked frantically to save Jonah's life.

* * *

The hospital waiting room was empty apart from an elderly couple seated beside the far window, so Robyn, Kim and Gabby sat down on the hideous beige couch along the wall. Doctors and nurses were attending to Jonah as they had been for the last forty-five minutes, but Robyn wasn't leaving until his condition improved. Mr. and Mrs. Parker were standing in the hallway, speaking to a female doctor in a stylish red pantsuit, and when the trio disappeared into Jonah's room, Robyn knew it was as good a time as any to come clean to her friends.

Fear gripped her heart, but Robyn was determined to have a frank, honest talk with Kim and Gabby. This conversation was long overdue, and Robyn knew if she chickened out now she'd never have the courage to tell them the truth.

Before she could confess, Kim spoke up. "I think Jaxon and I should postpone our wedding until Jonah's better."

"Jonah would hate that," Robyn replied. "He's always preaching to us about how precious love is and how we shouldn't hesitate when we find it. He'd want you to marry Jaxon as planned."

"Robyn's right," Gabby said, glancing up from her cell phone. "Besides, it's too late to cancel. I've already bought thousands of dollars' worth of veal, so don't even *think* of it."

As her friends debated the issue, Robyn felt as if she would bust. Now that she'd made up her mind to tell them, she couldn't hold it in any longer. She parted her lips, and the truth came tumbling out. "I've been secretly dating Sean for the past three weeks."

Kim spoke through pursed lips. "Sean who?"

Gabby shrieked. "Hot damn! I knew you had a lover, but I had no idea it was Sean. No wonder you've got a permanent smile on your face these days."

"How did you know I was seeing someone?"

"Because you suck at lying," Gabby said with a laugh. "Robyn, we've been friends forever, and I probably know you better than you know yourself."

"I thought I was being careful."

"Of course you did, but I'm your bestie, and I don't miss a thing." She gave Robyn a wink. "I put two and two together when you started skipping Pilates class and leaving the resort every night after work."

Kim shot to her feet. "I can't believe this! Of all the people you could have dated, why does it have to be him? Why couldn't you find someone else?"

"Because she's been crushing on Sean since they were teenagers, that's why." Gabby gave Robyn a one-arm hug and held her tight. "I'm *so* happy for you. You guys are perfect for each other, and I'm thrilled you finally found your one true love."

"Thanks, Gabby," she whispered, moved by her friend's words of encouragement. "Your support means more to me than you will ever know."

"Anytime, girl. That's what friends are for."

But Kim didn't have the same reaction. "How could you do this to me? You're supposed to be my best friend."

"I wanted to tell you sooner, but I didn't know how." A tremendous weight had been lifted off her shoulders by coming clean, but it tore her up inside to see her friend in pain. "Kim, I'm sorry. I should have told you about Sean from the beginning. He wanted me to, but I was scared of losing you as a friend, and I couldn't imagine my life without you."

"Save your apology for someone who cares," she shot back. "You've been running around with Sean behind my back and lying to me for weeks, and you have the nerve to sit there and act like everything's okay? Well, it's not. You betrayed me, and for all I know, you could be in cahoots with Sean to destroy the Belleza."

Robyn felt like a knife had been plunged into her heart, but she didn't lash back, didn't argue. Kim was upset, and rightfully so. In time, Robyn hoped her best friend would come around, because she was reuniting with Sean, and no one was going to stop her. In the meantime, she knew what she had to do.

"I don't want to cause you or anyone else at the resort undue stress," she said somberly, "so I'll tender my resignation first thing tomorrow."

"Tender your resignation?" Gabby repeated, her voice filled with confusion. "But you love working at the Belleza. You said it's the best job you've ever had."

"It is, but I don't want to hurt Kim any more than I already have." Her eyes stung with unshed tears.

"You can have Sean, your career *and* our friendship," Gabby insisted. "Right, Kim?"

"I don't know…" Kim trailed off.

"I never dreamed in a million years I'd find my soul mate, but I did. And now that I have Sean, I have everything I could ever want. Life is simply too short for regrets, and I'll never forgive myself if I lose the only man who's ever loved me unconditionally." *It had taken Jonah to make her understand that.* She gave a bittersweet smile as she thought of her dear friend, fighting for his life. Once again, he'd given her sage advice.

She started to get up from the couch, but she saw a police officer walk down the hall and meet up with the

Parkers, who'd just exited Jonah's room. What was he doing there?

"Sorry to interrupt, Mr. and Mrs. Parker," she heard him say, "but there's been a break in the case, and I'd like us to discuss the latest developments before someone leaks the information to the press."

The trio walked into the waiting room, and introductions were made. Robyn regarded the officer with open contempt. The surly detective had it out for Sean, and that made him enemy number one. If he said anything disparaging about her man, she was going to let him have it.

"Have you arrested the person responsible for Jonah's accident?" Robyn asked, cutting to the chase. "Are they finally in police custody?"

"Yes, and it's the last person any of you would have suspected." Detective Fenton sat down on one of the padded chairs, gestured for Mr. and Mrs. Parker to have a seat, and after they had, he continued. "Charlene Vincent confessed that she was hired by a third party to provide them with unlimited access to the grounds."

"What?" Kim, Gabby and Robyn shouted in unison. "Are you sure?"

"Yes. Charlene turned herself in when she realized that she was indirectly responsible for Jonah's accident. Sobbing hysterically, she admitted she never would have agreed to anything that would harm such a nice, sweet man."

"Who hired Charlene?" Mr. Parker asked solemnly. "Was it…my son?"

"No, sir, it wasn't. The third party turned out to be Trina Erickson."

Mrs. Parker gasped. "Sean's ex-girlfriend? But she's such a sweet girl."

"And an heiress, too," Kim added, her tone filled with righteous indignation.

"Trina is a major investor in The Pinnacle," Detective Fenton explained. "Apparently, she promised Charlene a position at her resort in the entertainment department and hefty financial compensation in exchange for her assistance."

"Why would Trina try to destroy the Belleza? What have we ever done to her?"

"Trina was outraged when your son broke up with her, Mrs. Parker, and felt that it wasn't enough for The Pinnacle to succeed. She wanted the Belleza to fall apart, and if Sean was arrested, the better. She found Charlene to be an easy pawn and played her for a fool."

Robyn thought back over the last three months, reflected on everything that had happened during the summer at the resort. She couldn't believe that Charlene—the hostess she'd befriended, and trusted—had plotted with Trina Erickson to destroy the Belleza. "Has Charlene been formally charged?" she asked, curious about what would happen to the young woman. Charlene was a good person who'd made a bad decision, and Robyn couldn't help but feel bad for her misguided coworker. "Is she looking at significant jail time?"

"I can't say for sure. We'll see what the DA thinks," Detective Fenton said. "A lot hinges on whether or not Jonah pulls through.

Kimberly narrowed her gaze. "Charlene is just as guilty as Trina, if not more. We trusted her."

"That's true," Detective Fenton conceded. "But Charlene had no idea Trina would attempt murder. What she thought would be a simple business maneuver turned into something ugly, but she was too scared to go to the police. Trina, on the other hand, is responsible for everything—the fire, the kitchen accidents and, most horrifyingly, the accident that severely injured Jonah Grady."

"I feel like an idiot," Mr. Parker confessed, hanging his head. "Charlene told me Sean resented me and how unhappy he was working at The Pearl, and I believed her. I bet they were all lies, just stories she made up to cause strife and dissention in our family."

"Yeah, Dad, they were. Every single one."

At the sound of that male voice, Robyn glanced to the right and spotted Sean as he entered the waiting room with Ryan. Her heart skipped two beats, and hope surged through her veins. Looking at Sean, she felt butterflies dance in the pit of her stomach. Robyn drank him up, openly stared at him. She loved the simplicity of his look, how attractive he looked in his fitted white shirt and jeans. They'd broken up twenty-four hours ago, but it felt like weeks since she'd seen him, touched him, enjoyed the pleasure of his kiss. Robyn wanted to go to Sean to apologize for the things she'd said last night but knew it wasn't the right time.

"Sean! Ryan! It's so good to see you!" Mrs. Parker jumped to her feet and threw her arms around her sons. "My babies are finally home!"

Robyn watched in amusement as Ilene hugged and kissed her sons as if they were school-aged children rather than grown men. It was a heartwarming moment.

Robyn tried to catch Sean's eye, but he looked right through her, as if she wasn't there. A searing pain shot through her heart, made her body numb with cold. He was mad at her, no doubt about it, and Robyn didn't blame him; she'd messed up big time. She had her work cut out for her, trying to convince him she'd made a terrible mistake, but she was determined to win him back. Nothing scared her more than the thought of being without him. Her desire for him was so strong, so powerful, she couldn't stop staring at him.

"I'm so glad you're back in the Belleza. I've been waiting for this day for eight long months."

"It's good to be home." Ryan kissed his mom on the cheek. "Now, what's for supper?"

Everyone laughed, and the tension in the air lifted.

"How is Jonah doing?" Sean asked.

Sadness filled Mrs. Parker's eyes. "Doctors are with him now, but it doesn't look good."

"I owe you an apology, Sean," Detective Fenton said, his tone contrite.

"That makes two of us." Mr. Parker stood and joined his wife. "I'm sorry for ever doubting you, son, and I hope one day you can forgive me."

Slowly nodding his head, Sean stepped forward and shook the hand his dad offered.

"We've never been close, but I'd like us to have a better relationship," Kurt Parker said.

A grin lit Sean's face. "I'd like that, too, old man."

"So would I."

Kim rose to her feet, crossed the room toward her family, and stopped in front of Sean. Tears pooled in her eyes and spilled down her face. "I know you hate me, but I miss you, and it would mean the world to me to have you at my wedding."

"What are you talking about, silly? I could never hate you." Sean cleaned the tears from her cheeks and pulled her into his open arms. "I was an ass, and I'm sorry."

"You're right. You were." Kim laughed. "Apology accepted."

Sean kissed her forehead. "I love you, sis."

"And I love you more."

"Hey! What's up with that?" Ryan piped up, his hand over his heart as if he'd been mortally wounded. "I thought *I* was your favorite!"

Everyone in the room laughed, and Robyn wondered if anyone would be able to tame the aspiring musician with the bad-boy ways. Ryan was a jokester, and there was never a dull moment when he was around.

"Sean, you'd better treat Robyn like a queen or else you'll have to answer to me," Gabby said, pointing a thumb at her chest. "I'm serious. If you hurt her in any way, you're dead meat."

"Robyn?" Mr. and Mrs. Parker said in unison, sharing a puzzled look. "Can someone please tell us what's going on? We're lost."

"Allow me." Robyn stood, took her rightful place beside Sean and intertwined her fingers with his. His body stiffened, and his eyes widened in surprise. Robyn maintained her smile, didn't let her disappointment show on her face. She wished things had been different, that she'd faced her fears head-on instead of pushing Sean away, but she was ready to prove her love, right here, right now. "Sean and I are a couple, and we're getting married next year."

"We are?" he asked, giving her a sideways glance, a frown wedged between his lips. "You told me you weren't ready for a serious relationship, and I respect your decision."

En masse, everyone slipped away, leaving them alone.

"I'm confused," he confessed. "Last night you walked out on me, and now you're talking marriage."

Robyn faced him. "We can fix things, Sean, I know we can."

"How, when we want different things?"

"I need you in my life, for the rest of my life, and I'll do anything to make things right."

"Why the sudden change of heart? What happened to bring this about?"

Her lips were painfully dry, and it hurt to swallow, but Robyn found the courage to answer his question. "I was running scared for years, but a wise old man taught me something today. Jonah made me realize how short life is, how precious it is, and I can't live another minute without you. I'm ready to start a new chapter of my life, and the only man I want to love and live and laugh with is you."

"For how long? A few weeks? A couple months? Until you find Mr. Right?"

"No, baby, forever. And make no doubt about it, *you* are Mr. Right."

Silence fell between them, and Robyn feared all was lost.

"How do I know you won't walk out on me again? Or push me away?

"Because you have my word." Robyn hadn't known she had it in her, but she spoke openly, without fear or restraint. She told Sean everything that was in her heart. "You asked me where I see myself in five years, but I was too scared to tell you the truth."

"And the truth is?"

"I want to marry you and have kids and live in the suburbs."

Sean wore an arch grin, and Robyn knew she was finally making progress with him.

"Anything else I should know?" he asked her.

"I promise to love you in good times and bad for as long as we both shall live."

"Are you proposing to me, Ms. Henderson?"

"Yes, if that's what it takes to prove my love. I need you in my life, Sean, and I won't live without you." Robyn took his hand, placed it on her chest and covered it with her own. "You have my heart, and that will never, ever change, not even when we're old and gray."

"Baby, I love the sound of that," he whispered, brushing his nose against hers. "I love you, Robyn, and I can't wait to make you my lawfully wedded wife."

Giddy with excitement, she looped her arms around his neck and moved in for a kiss.

"Everyone's watching us," he whispered, gesturing into the hallway with a flick of his head. "And I'm pretty sure Gabby's recording us on her cell phone."

"That's fine by me, because I want the whole world to know that you're my man." To prove it, Robyn pressed her body against his and kissed him passionately on the lips. His mouth was sweet and intoxicating, his caress thrilling, and his whispered promises made her heart overflow with love. They clung desperately to each other, like a couple lost at sea, and when Robyn heard muted applause from the hallway, she knew they had the support of their friends and family. *Thanks, Jonah,* she thought, snuggling against Sean's chest. *You were right. There is nothing worth more than love.*

Chapter 16

"You've planned dozens of high-profile events over the years, but this charity gala takes the cake—literally," Mrs. Parker gushed as she held up a forkful of a masterful raspberry torte. She tasted it, and her eyes went wide. Her voice was filled with awe when she continued, complimenting Robyn, "I don't think I've ever attended a more lavish, elegant party, and I've been to state dinners at the White House!"

"I second that." Mr. Parker nodded his head in agreement. "You went above and beyond your job description, and because of your remarkable efforts, dozens of guests have expressed interest in hosting similar events at the Belleza in the near future."

Humbled by the couple's praise, Robyn smiled her thanks. The entire Parker family except for Ryan, who was onstage, was seated around the table, enjoying cocktails, spirited conversation and the live music. The new-lyweds, Kim and Jaxon, were whispering in each other's ears, and Gabby was feeding Geoffrey hand-dipped chocolate truffles. Her girlfriends wowed in floor-length black gowns, and their men looked dapper in tailored Armani suits.

It had taken months of planning, and now that the Dunham Foundation gala was winding down, Robyn could finally breathe a sigh of relief. Glancing around the restaurant, she assessed the work her team had done. The Pearl had been transformed into a magical, enchanted space, one as unique as it was breathtaking. Round tables were outfitted with designer linens, sparkling china and potted candles that smelled of lemon blossoms, but it was the towering centerpieces, overflowing with ivory roses, hydrangeas and orchids, which gave the venue its ethereal feel.

"Can I interest you in something to drink? Perhaps an espresso or chamomile tea?"

Robyn smiled politely at the tuxedo-clad waiter but shook her head. Dinner had been a feast, an elaborate five-course meal full of flavor, and three hours later, guests were still raving about the scrumptious food. Politicians, business tycoons and A-list celebrities were in attendance, mingling, socializing and posing for pictures. Ryan was performing a medley of Motown hits with his all-female band, and couples draped in jewels and Givenchy were heating things up on the dance floor.

At the table, Mrs. Parker was still gushing. "I still don't know how you managed to pull this off, what with Sean's grand opening, Kim's wedding *and* visiting Jonah at the hospital, but let me be the first to say that this is the best charity gala the Belleza has ever had."

"Thank you, Mrs. Parker, but I didn't do this alone. It was a team effort, and everyone from the kitchen staff to the waiters and sound technicians played a part in making the night a success." Robyn winked at her future in-laws. "Your seven-figure donation didn't hurt, either."

At the conclusion of the program, as guests were enjoying their dessert, Mr. and Mrs. Parker had taken to the stage and graciously thanked everyone for supporting the Dunham Foundation. Shocking everyone in attendance, the couple had pledged a million dollars to the cause and promised to work side by side with the foundation to help impoverished families in their beloved state. Two million dollars had been raised in less than three hours, making the charity gala the most successful event in the Belleza history.

"I agree with Mom," Sean added. "You did an amazing job at Jaxon and Kim's wedding last Saturday, but you really outdid yourself tonight." Draping an arm around her shoulders, he leaned over and kissed Robyn on the cheek. "See, Mom, you got your wish after all. I'm marrying a smart, successful woman just like you."

His words made Robyn grin from ear to ear. Every time she thought of marrying Sean, her heart swelled with joy. *This time next year, I'll be Mrs. Sean Parker. How awesome is that?*

Her thoughts returned to Labor Day, to the exact moment her life had changed forever. On the morning of the grand opening of the SP Grill, Robyn had woken up to breakfast in bed and a romantic, heartfelt proposal. It was a sweet, intimate moment, and for as long as she lived, she'd never forget how special Sean had made her feel. And when he'd dropped to one knee and slipped the emerald-cut diamond on her ring finger, she'd kissed him with all the passion and heat she felt for him.

After making love, they'd driven to Palm Springs and shared the happy news with her mother. It was there, while celebrating over appetizers and champagne, that her dad had called. Robyn had been stunned to discover Sean had flown to New York days earlier and met with her dad at his Manhattan apartment. The two men had talked for hours, and at the end of their conversation, Sean had asked for her hand in marriage. In that phone call to Robyn, her dad had apologized for being an absentee father, and since that afternoon, they'd talked several times. Robyn didn't know if they'd ever be close or if they'd have the father-daughter relationship she'd always dreamed of, but it was a start. She choked up every time she thought about what Sean had done for her, and thanked her lucky stars that they'd reconciled and were now engaged.

"Sean, I couldn't agree more. I'm thrilled that you guys are a couple, but don't prolong your engagement," Mrs. Parker advised, her tone matter-of-fact. "I'm ready for grandbabies, and you're my only hope, so hurry up and tie the knot already."

"Your only hope?" Sean repeated. "What about Kim and Jaxon?"

"Kim said they're not ready to start a family, and since Ryan would rather sow his wild oats than settle down, I'm depending on you."

"One sweet, adorable grandchild coming right up, Mom!"

Robyn burst out laughing. They were planning a small, intimate wedding at The Pearl on Valentine's Day, but

Robyn was so anxious to become Mrs. Sean Parker she was considering bumping up the date.

"I saw the review for the SP Grill in the *LA Times* this morning. Congrats, man." Geoffrey raised his champagne glass to Sean in salute. "Your restaurant's only been open a few weeks, but it's already the toast of the town. Need another investor?"

"Have your people call my people," Sean said with a chuckle. "I can't take any of the credit. Robyn's brilliant ideas and Ryan's outstanding performance helped make the grand opening a success. That's why I hired them both to work for me on a permanent basis."

The light in Kim's eyes faded, but she was grinning. "You don't have to rub it in, Sean."

Robyn wore a half smile as she listened to her fiancé and her best friend argue over her. She was going to miss working at the resort full-time, but she was excited about helping Sean run the SP Grill. They made a great team, and she loved working side by side with him. Her happiest moments were laughing and joking around with him in the kitchen, and Robyn was looking forward to the next chapter of their lives.

The moment Robyn heard the opening verse of "I'm Every Woman," she jumped up, dragged Kim and Gabby to their feet and led them through the crowd. Finding a spot at the foot of the stage, they danced, giggled and sang off-key.

Watching her girlfriends cut loose on the dance floor, Robyn marveled at how much their lives had changed over the summer. Kim and Jaxon had married last Saturday in a lavish ceremony attended by three hundred friends and family members and were leaving on their honeymoon tomorrow morning, and Gabby was so blissfully in love with Geoffrey she talked about him nonstop. Recently, she'd joked about them eloping in Bermuda during the Christmas holidays, and Robyn wouldn't be surprised if they did.

Twirling around, she spotted her fiancé a few feet behind her and danced into his arms. Sean looked handsome in his crisp white tuxedo, every bit as sexy as the Hollywood stars milling around the room.

"You're the most beautiful woman in here."

A girlish smile overwhelmed her mouth. To please him, she'd worn the strapless purple gown he'd bought her while shopping in Venice Beach weeks earlier, and feeling his hands along the soft satin material made her body flush with heat. He splayed kisses on her cheeks and neck, stroked her shoulders and hips, arousing her flesh. They swayed to the beat of the music, moved their bodies sensuously against each other. They danced to song after song, flirted and laughed like teenagers at a high school dance. The air was charged with sexual tension, and thoughts of making love consumed her mind till she could no longer take the sweet torture.

"Are you thinking what I'm thinking?" Sean asked, tickling her ear with the tip of his tongue. "Because if you are, I know the perfect place for a quickie."

"I thought you'd never ask," she quipped, her words a breathless pant. "Let's go!"

Sean took Robyn's hand, but before they could flee The Pearl, Kim grabbed his arm and led them outside. The breeze was warm, perfumed with a floral fragrance, and the sky was awash with hundreds of twinkling stars. Ryan's silky, smooth voice flowed through the doors, creating a romantic mood. They sat down at a candlelit table with Jaxon and Gabby and Geoffrey, and as they chatted about the highlights of the evening, Robyn's thoughts turned to everyone's favorite bartender.

"I wish Jonah was here," she said with a sad smile. "He would've loved rubbing elbows with all of the Hollywood big shots tonight."

Gabby laughed. "You're right. He probably would have pitched his story about the Belleza treasure to every producer in there."

"The Belleza curse may not have been a real thing," Robyn said, "but the Belleza treasure sure was."

"It was?" Geoffrey cocked an eyebrow. "You're pulling my leg. Right, Robyn?"

Robyn glanced at Kim, and when she gave a nod of consent, she decided to tell Jaxon and Geoffrey what Jonah had whispered in her ear the day he thought he was dying. Thankfully, he'd survived the accident, but he would remain in the hospital until he recovered from his injuries. The doctors couldn't explain his sudden improvement, except to say he had a strong will to live. Everyone was taking turns visiting Jonah at the hospital, and he was in good spirits.

"Of course she's pulling your leg," Jaxon said. "The Belleza treasure is a myth."

"The treasure turned out to be an 18-carat blue diamond, and it wasn't actually on the property of the resort, but it was buried not too far from here," she began, not surprised by the bewildered expressions on their faces. The day of Trina's arrest, Robyn had told Kim and Gabby the truth about the treasure and had explained everything to Sean the morning he'd proposed, but it still blew her mind that Jonah—everyone's favorite bartender—was a multimillionaire.

"An 18-carat blue diamond?" Geoffrey leaned forward in his chair. "Go on, Robyn. I'm listening."

"Jonah's had the diamond stashed since the 1950s, but he never talked about it because it caused the breakup with his one true love. He wanted to keep the ring as a family heirloom to one day pass on to his children, but his wife wanted to sell it and live a life of luxury. They couldn't agree, and after years of arguing they decided to go their separate ways."

"That's sad. It's too bad Jonah couldn't have his wife, *and* the treasure," Jaxon said, his eyes filled with pity. "How did you know where to find the treasure, Robyn?"

"Jonah told me where to find it after he passed away and asked me to split the money three ways with Kim and Gabby. When he recovered, he still wanted us to have it."

Geoffrey's jaw dropped.

"I didn't believe the story, either, when Robyn first told me," Sean said, smiling sympathetically at his friend and brother-in-law. "But every word of it is true. I saw the diamond myself, and it's a thing of beauty."

Kim added, "I remember my grandpa Don telling me stories of the Belleza treasure when I was a kid. I always assumed they were fairy tales, but perhaps he knew more than he let on."

Jaxon shook his head. "I never would have guessed that Jonah was rich. He lives such a simple, modest life."

"Not anymore," Gabby said proudly. "We bought him one of the luxury staff condos and insisted he keep half the money so he could live comfortably. Kim forced him to retire, but I suspect he'll be sneaking into the Belleza to mix drinks at the bar when we're not looking."

Everyone shared a smile.

Geoffrey glanced conspicuously over his shoulder and

dropped his voice to a whisper. "Robyn, if you don't mind me asking, how much was the diamond worth? A million? Five million? *Ten* million?"

"Let's just say it was enough to make a significant donation to the Dunham Foundation and establish the Jonah Grady Scholarship at Merriweather Academy," Robyn said, feeling as if she was going to burst with pride. Kim and Gabby were beaming, too, and she knew her friends were as excited as she was. "Merriweather Academy had an enormous impact on my life, and if I hadn't won that scholarship, I never would have met my besties or my boo."

Everyone chuckled, and Robyn exploded into giggles when Sean nipped her earlobe.

"That's right, baby, I'm your boo, and you're stuck with me for life."

"I *love* the sound of that."

"And I love you." He kissed her then, slowly and thoughtfully. "You're the best thing that's ever happened to me, and I'll never take you or our love for granted."

He'd changed her way of thinking and proved he could be trusted with her heart. She'd come alive since they'd started dating and thrived on knowing she had his unconditional love and support, and as he whispered sweet nothings in her ear, she melted into his warm embrace.

Robyn glanced at her best friends and noted how beautiful they looked, how in love.

Kim's face was alight with happiness, and Gabby's eyes were so bright they could outshine the stars. They'd all found their soul mates, their true loves.

"I'd like to make a toast." Geoffrey grabbed the bottle of Cristal champagne in the ice bucket, popped it open and filled six glasses to the brim. "Here's to love, happiness and prosperity!"

The couples clinked glasses and drank their champagne.

Robyn and Sean spent the rest of the night outside with their friends, dancing in the light of the moon. And when Sean curled his arms around her waist and gave her a slow, sensuous kiss on the lips, Robyn knew all of her hopes and dreams had finally come true.

* * * * *

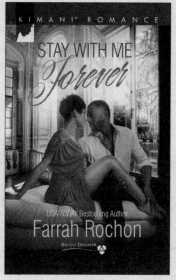
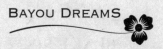

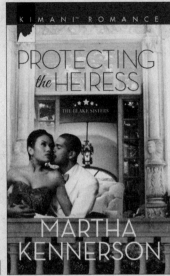

REQUEST YOUR FREE BOOKS!

2 FREE NOVELS
PLUS 2 FREE GIFTS!

KIMANI™
ROMANCE

Love's ultimate destination!

KROM15

BESTSELLING AUTHOR COLLECTION

CLASSIC ROMANCES IN COLLECTIBLE VOLUMES

New York Times **Bestselling Author**

BRENDA JACKSON

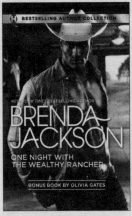

Sometimes a knight in shining armor wears a cowboy hat

Seven years ago, as a young cop, Darius Franklin saved a vulnerable woman from a violent situation. They shared one night of pure passion before she walked away. Now Darius is a wealthy rancher and security contractor working at a women's shelter. And he's shocked to meet the new social worker: Summer Martindale, a beautiful damsel no longer in distress.

ONE NIGHT WITH THE WEALTHY RANCHER